C0-AYI-722

AFRICAN WRITERS SERIES LIST

Founding editor · Chinua Achebe

AFRICAN WRITERS SERIES

147

The Horn of my Love

Here's some
home + high poem,
but for its a from
welcome Home

Okot p'Bitek

The Horn
of my Love

OKOT p'BITEK

LONDON
HEINEMANN
LUSAKA · NAIROBI · IBADAN

Heinemann Educational Books Ltd
48 Charles Street, London WIX 8AH
P.M.B. 5205, Ibadan · P.O. Box 45314,
Nairobi · P.O. Box 3966, Lusaka
EDINBURGH MELBOURNE TORONTO
AUCKLAND NEW DELHI SINGAPORE
HONG KONG KUALA LUMPUR

ISBN 0 435 90147 8

Printed in Great Britain by
Richard Clay (The Chaucer Press) Ltd
Bungay, Suffolk

Contents

Preface

When, recently, my friend Taban lo Liyong wept bitter tears over what he called *the literary desert in East Africa*, he was suffering from acute literary deafness, a disease which afflicts those who have been brainwashed to believe that literature exists only in books. Taban and his fast dwindling clan are victims of the class-ridden, dictionary meaning of the term *literature*, which restricts literary activity and enjoyment to the so-called literate peoples, and turns a deaf ear to the songs and stories of the vast majority of our people in the countryside. In this book I have presented the poetry of Taban's own people, the Acoli of northern Uganda.

Missionaries, anthropologists, musicologists and folklorists have shown some professional interest in the oral literature of African peoples. They have plucked songs, stories, proverbs, riddles etc. from their social backgrounds and, after killing them by analysis, have buried them in inaccessible and learned journals and in expensive technical books. I believe that literature, like all the other creative arts, is there, first and foremost, to be enjoyed. Here is the poetry of the Acoli people: their lullabies and love songs, their satirical verses, their religious songs and chants, their war songs and funeral dirges. Going through them we may get a glimpse of what these people think and believe life is all about; their moral values, their sense of humour, their fears and joys are presented here in these songs.

The book is divided into three parts. In Part One I have discussed briefly the different dances or occasions when the songs are sung. The ceremonies of the spirit possession dance and the sacrifices to the ancestors are described in my book, *Religion of the Central Luo* (East African Literature Bureau, Nairobi). Part Two consists of the texts, both in the Acoli language and in English. It is important to stress that these are my own translations, and I believe that there can be other versions. It is for this reason that the vernacular had to be included, to give other translators and scholars the opportunity to criticise my translation and also to attempt their own. In Part Three I have thrown together several items ranging from analysis of the themes in Acoli dirges, the role of poets as historians, a description of the so-called 'praise name', and a rendering of the warriors' titles.

I learnt many of these songs as I grew up, and my first thanks go to my mother Lacwaa, a composer, dancer and one-time leader of the girls in Palaro chiefdom, who taught me a considerable number of songs. Secondly, I want to thank my age-mates and companions, especially Acamu Lubwa Too, Abonga Bongomin Lutwala, Odida, Okelo Antonio, Oloya Acil, Lawoko wod Okelo and numerous other friends, for the joy we all shared at the dance arenas, at the *nanga* parties, and especially during the Gulu festivals. From the elder generation of poets and musicians, the late Yona Ocwaa, Omal Adok Too, Goya and Oryema Erenayo, I learnt the older songs, and they deserve special thanks.

From 1960 to 1963 I carried out research among the Acoli and Lango, and a word of gratitude goes to my teacher and friend, Godfrey Lienhardt, who supervised the work. Gerald Moore, one-time director of the Extra-Mural Department at Makerere took a keen interest in the poetry of the Acoli people; I am grateful for his friendship and help. Lastly, I want to pay tribute to my colleagues in the University of Nairobi, especially Ngugi wa Thiong'o, Taban lo Liyong and Owuor Anyumba who a few years back started the literary revolution which demolished the English Department and replaced it with the Department of Literature, the central core of which is African literature. This book is a contribution to that revolution.

OKOT p'BITEK
NAIROBI

PART I

Children's games and songs[1]

The poetry of Acoli children—aged from three to about thirteen—comprises lullabies, play-songs and counts. A lullaby (Nos. 1 and 2) is sung by a *lapidi*, nurse, who is usually an older sister or brother of the baby. Mothers also sing lullabies to their babies. Held in the arm, or strapped on the back, the baby is swayed gently, and this is accompanied by the singing of the lullaby. The soothing effect of this sends the baby to sleep.

Acoli children have a large repertoire of games, and most of them are accompanied by singing. For example, *Dini-dini ye* (No. 5) is a 'hide and seek' game. A little boy or girl kneels before the 'referee' who drums his or her back quite hard with his fists, while singing the solo. The rest of the children take up the chorus and dance to the rhythm of the 'drum'. The singing and dancing stops when the referee sings *Lamanya-manya puk*, and closes the eyes of the 'drum'; and the rest of the children run and hide themselves. When the 'drum's' eyes are opened, he endeavours to chase and touch any of the other children before they return to the spot where the referee is standing. The child who is touched becomes the next 'drum'. Should the 'drum' fail to touch anybody, he again provides the 'drum' for the next round. In *Okutu oryang*[2] (No. 6) the girls line up before the boys and, as they sing, they all dance and move close to each other and then move away, and so on. In *Lililili Lango obino* (No. 8) a circle is formed by joining hands tightly; a soloist who is in the middle of the circle starts to sing and everybody joins the chorus, and they all move very fast in an anticlockwise direction. Suddenly, the soloist shouts *Lililic*, and all fall to the ground at once. The last person to fall down becomes the next soloist.

The *count* is a game in which words are used instead of figures. *Min latin* (No. 10) counts to ten:

Min	latin	ocito	kulu	onongo	lwango	opong	te	latin	bic
1	2	3	4	5	6	7	8	9	10

[1] For a detailed study of Acoli childhood see Anna Apoko, 'At Home in the Village: Growing up in Acoli', in Lorene K. Fox (ed.), *East African Childhood*, Nairobi, 1967.
[2] The thorn of the *oryang* tree is a euphemism for penis.

As they repeat this poem, the children indicate the counting on their fingers or toes. *Awiyo tolla* (No. 11) counts up to seventy-one. The players sit down in a line and stretch both of their legs out in front of them. The counter starts at one end of the line and moves along the line, touching each leg: one leg per word of the poem. At the end of the song, the last leg to be touched is folded. Then the counter starts to count from the next leg, and this goes on until all the legs have been folded, or until the children are tired of the game.

The lullabies, the games and the songs accompanying them form a most important introduction to the cultural and moral education of the Acoli child. As he participates in these enjoyable activities, he learns to express himself through his body movement, in his voice as he sings, and in the poetry. He develops his sense of rhythm as he keeps in time with the rest—a very significant training for the complex dances, music and poetry of the adults. The child is plunged right into the core of poetry, which is the song that arises from the tensions of human interaction. In *Min latin*, for instance, we hear the child commenting on his mother's apparent politeness while she is still busy, and her apparent rudeness after she has finished her chores. In *Awiyo tolla* (No. 11) we see the quality of self-reliance and self-confidence being inculcated.

Furthermore, the child begins to learn the attitude of his people to death and other matters. To the Acoli, the death of a very old person is not considered a terribly sad thing. *In Dini-dini ye* (No. 5) we hear the children making fun of the death of one such old woman who had overstayed her welcome in this world. And in *Okutu oryang* (No. 6) sex is treated not as something to be ashamed of, but as a good thing to be enjoyed.

History is introduced in such games as *Luduku pa Langalanga* (No. 4). Langalanga is the nickname the Acoli gave to Captain (later Brigadier-General Sir) Charles Delme-Radcliffe, a British soldier-imperialist, who arrived in Acoliland in 1898, and forced or bribed many Acoli chiefs to thumb so-called treaties of protection.[3] A harsh and ruthless man, gifted with brilliant marksmanship, he covered vast distances, travelling mainly by night. Langalanga means 'lion'. In *Lililili Lango obino* (No. 8) the children are introduced to the feud that existed

[3] See Lacito Okech, *Tekwaro ki ker lobo Acoli*, Kampala, 1953, p. 24, and R. M. Bere, 'Awich—A biographical note and chapter of Acoli History', *Uganda Journal*, Vol. 10, No. 2, Sept. 1949.

between their people and the Lango.[4] The game is also an exercise in what to do if and when the enemy attack.

It is interesting that when the children are engaged in these games and dances they are always alone; they organise themselves without the aid of adults. To begin with, these games usually take place during the working hours of the day, when the grown-ups are away in the fields, hoeing, weeding or harvesting; the grown-up boys and girls accompany the adults to the fields or take the cattle, goats or sheep to feed in the wild pastures; during the dry season the elders attend hunts and go on safaris. The children left at home spend the day playing and singing.

Indeed, any grown-up boy or girl who may be tempted to join the children in their games is rebuked and told, '*In pe latin, imono ka tuku i kweyo.*' 'You are no longer a child, you should be ashamed of playing in the sand.'[5] 'And, of course, children always want to feel that they are grown up; a boy of about thirteen years of age would cry bitterly if he were prevented from accompanying the grown-ups.

One question arises as to the composers of these children's poems and the origin of the dances and games. Some of them are obviously quite old, and so we may say that these songs were handed down from generation to generation of children. But this does not answer our question; moreover, this kind of statement is part and parcel of the view of folklorists, which in our opinion is incorrect, that folk music and songs have no individual composers, but simply emerge from the crowd. In the Acoli context every song, every tune, had an individual and original composer. Of course, the song may be modified by another singer to suit his own particular mood or situation; singing and dancing are creative processes, and no one ever sings exactly like another person. This, however, does not remove the fact that songs have their original composers.

[4] For a description of Acoli and Lango wars see N. Latigo, 'Mony ma con i kom rok murumu Acoli' (Wars of old on the peoples whose countries bordered Acoliland), in *Acoli Magazine* No. 3, 1947; A. Tarantino, 'Lango wars', in *Uganda Journal*, Vol. 10, No. 2, Sept. 1949.
[5] The following song is sung when a boy likes to stay in the kitchen instead of playing with other grown-up boys outside:

Odure, katti woko,	*Odure, come outside,*
Wat keno,	*Leave the cooking-place;*
Mac keno wango cuni, ah!	*Fire from the stove will burn your penis, ah!*

There is no doubt that the children compose their own songs and are their own choreographers. The more talented among them emerge as leaders of the games and as soloists, but, this being a team activity, everyone joins in, enjoying themselves creatively, while at the same time imbibing the culture and values of their society.

Orak—the love dance

Orak is the most informal dance of the Acoli people, in that there is no special occasion for it, and to hold it no chief's authority or permission is required. Usually, however, it is held in connection with marriage, and so it is also called *myel keny*, marriage dance. Thus when a girl has been abducted, *opor*, that is when she has left her home secretly with her lover,[1] the dance is held nightly until her people come to take her back. And again during the payment of bridewealth and the completion of marriage ceremonies the dance is performed for days. After a communal co-operative cultivation of a garden or the construction of a house, beer is consumed, and later in the night, *orak* is danced.

Within a short period of about fifty years this dance has undergone many changes and has assumed various names. Lacito Okech has written that around 1906 it was called *ajere*.[2] This name persisted in some parts of Acoliland until 1923 when it became known as *lalobolobo*. According to Rene M. Bere, '. . . all the dancers carry little sticks. The men form an outer ring of a circle, and the girls the inner ring. There are no drums at all in this dance and the movements are rather slow and stiff . . . Beer is not made and there are no special occasions for the dance.'[3] The small sticks were beaten to produce the rhythm. Following this the dance became known as *lacele*, and afterwards as *lacukucuku*. This was the time when *lacukucuku*, a kind of rattle, made out of the fruit of a plant known by that name was introduced. The inside of the fruit, which is about an inch in diameter, is scooped out, and small stones are put inside. Three to twelve of these are then joined together by a string which is tied around the leg. The rattle jingles as the dancer stamps the ground rhythmically.

The following song, calling *lacukucuku* a poor man's ankle bells, was composed at that time.

Gara pa lacan lacuku do,	*Ankle bells of the poor oh,*
Gara pa lacan ye,	*It is the ankle bells of the poor ;*
Lacukucuku, kati woko,	*He who has lacukucuku, do not be shy, come out ;*

[1] See James Obol-Ochola, 'Abduction', *East Africa Law Journal*, Vol. 3, 1967.
[2] Lacito Okech, *Te Kwaro ki ker lobo Acholi*, Kampala, 1953, p. 20.
[3] Rene M. Bere, 'Acoli dances', *Uganda Journal*, Vol. 1, No. 1, 1934, p. 61.

Gara pa lacan do;	*It is the ankle bells of the poor oh,*
Gara pa lacan, lacuku do,	*It is the ankle bells of the poor, lacuku oh,*
Gara pa lacan omera,	*It is the ankle bells of the poor, brother,*
Lacukucuku kati woko.	*He who has lacukucuku do not be shy, come out.*

In some parts of Acoliland dancers wore a thing called *lalimu*, a headdress on which is mounted a ball, fitted at the end of a stick about a foot long. As they stamped the ground rhythmically, the dancers shook their heads so that the ball moved up and down. It is difficult to do this and sing at the same time. So those who wore *lalimu* danced silently. And so the dance came to be called *lalingo-lingo*, silent dance.

Quite recently a man called Larakaraka introduced new styles and movements. Instead of the little sticks mentioned by Bere, he initiated the use of half gourds, *awal*, which were tapped rhythmically by a bunch of small sticks tied together. Today bicycle spokes are used. The new movement was called by the name of the initiator. It is recorded in the following song.

Larakaraka okelo myel me deyo,	*Larakaraka has brought a new dance of beauty,*
Larakaraka oroto myel me deyo . . .	*Larakaraka has invented a new dance of beauty . . .*

Orak is the short form of *larakaraka*. When performed in the night by moonlight it is called *lamoko owang* or *omok* for short. One type of millet beer called *labwor* is made from baked millet-flour. The story goes that one girl who was baking the flour could not resist the throbbing of the drums. She left the flour on the cooking-stove and went off to the dance. The flour was ruined by the fire, *moko owang;* hence the name.

The *orak* is primarily a dance for youths. Adults are virtually prohibited from joining in, although they may watch from the edge of the arena and, when highly provoked, old women dance in a circle around the arena. Young married women are strictly forbidden, for, as Anywar has called it, this is *myel cuna*, dance for wooing.[4] It is important to bear this in mind when we consider the meanings of the love songs and the satirical verses. Because, in the presence of a lover and

[4] Anywar, *Acoli ki ker megi*, Kampala, 1954, p. 211.

6

a rival, criticism, accusations and insults tend to be sharper and to cut more deeply than in other circumstances.

The dance is attended by young men and women from the locality that is, those living within a few hours' walk from the arena. But the dancers come from different clan groups. The youths meet and get to know one another. They discover possible future mates or strengthen existing relationships.

On nearing the arena, a party of dancers from one village splits into two: the girls move off in a group to join another group of men from another village. For in this dance a man may not have as a partner his sister, niece, aunt or any relative, that is, anyone he is prohibited from marrying. The main reason is that the dance provides an opportunity to meet prospective spouses. But another important reason is that some of the songs are quite obscene, and it is not proper to sing such songs in the presence of one's female relatives, and vice versa. The following are two such songs:

Ginni mit ki wor do,	*This thing is sweet at night oh,*
Tun mit ka lucubu ngete;	*Vagina is sweet when speared on the sides;*
Tun mit aba wor,	*Vagina is sweet at night,*
Aba wor lwenyo kene ye;	*Those active at night struggle alone oh,*
Myel opong ki wor ye,	*There is a big dance at night ee,*
Ginni mit ki wor.	*This thing is sweet at night.*
Miya mo do,	*Give it to me oh,*
Ginni gire tum ku;	*That thing does not wear out;*
Miya abil ba,	*Let me taste it oh,*
Ginni gire telo;	*This thing is erect;*
Kel abil do,	*Bring it, let me taste it,*
Ladeng bene telo.	*The clitoris is also erect.*

The entrance by a newly arrived group is resisted by the people already occupying the arena. A soloist from the new group starts a song, leaping in the air and playing on his half gourd. Members of his group take up the chorus. This is met by disruptive jeers, shouts and counter songs from the other groups. If the new group is thus discouraged, it is a great shame, and girls who had come to join them move away. If they succeed in getting the rest of the dancers to join in their song and dance to it, this is considered great success and a matter of pride.

The young men in a curved line interlock their legs, bend forward and play on their half gourds as they sing and move their bodies to the rhythm of the drums. The girls lined up before the boys swing their bodies in the movement called *piyo teke*. There are a number of songs about girls who cannot do this so well.

Lanyanni wiro dude awira,	*This woman merely turns her buttocks,*
Nya pa twon	*The daughter of the bull*
Teke dong peke;	*Cannot dance the teke;*
Nen, lakome wac,	*Behold the lazy one,*
Wiro dude awira.	*Merely turns her buttocks.*

If the young man is pleased with the performance of any girl, he leaves his place in the line and holds her right hand high, while whispering a few words of love in her ears.

The drums have different tunes, varying with the different drummers. There are usually four drums, three small ones, called *lakele*, and the big one called *min bul*, mother drum.

The dance breaks up unannounced. Parties from the different villages leave as and when they please, but there is much chasing of girls in the bushes. The *orak* compares with the dance of the youths of Buganda which, John Roscoe recorded, 'took place nightly amidst the plantain groves during the time when the moon was nearing full and especially on nights of full moon. The wives of the King and chiefs were strictly prohibited to take part. The mixed dances ended frequently in immoral conduct.'[5]

Commenting on the dance songs of the Ila-speaking people of Zambia (formerly Northern Rhodesia), Smith and Dale arrogantly asserted, 'It is not easy, even for one well acquainted with the language, to translate these songs. They abound in words and phrases without any meaning, like "Hi-tiddly-hi-hi" .'[6] And Evans-Pritchard wrote of Azande poetry, 'All these songs have meanings but the degree of meaning varies. Their meaning is not doubtful in their creator's mind, for they refer to persons and events known to him. The meaning

[5] John Roscoe, *The Baganda*, London, 1911, p. 24.
[6] E. B. Smith and A. M. Dale, *The Ila-speaking peoples of Northern Rhodesia*, London, 1920 (2 vols), p. 272.

conveyed to those who sing or hear them depends upon the degree to which they are acquainted with the person or happenings referred to.' Then he added, 'Meaning in both its qualities of sound and sense undergoes many phonetic and grammatical changes. Generally speaking we can say that *it is the melody and not the sense which matters*, or, as we say in common parlance, *it is the tune which matters* and not the words.'[7]

The suggestion that the words of the songs are either meaningless or, that even if they mean something to a few people, it is the tune which matters and not the poem, must be completely rejected. There is no dance, except that of wizards, in which there is no singing. The rhythms of the drums and the half gourds alone do not make men dance. These, like the melody produced by the *nanga*, form the background to the Song.

The songs refer to persons and events known not only to the poet, but also to the social group. The dancers sing them because they are psychologically and sociologically significant. The poet is the agent of his society. He has the talent, which other members of his social group may not possess, of distilling the thoughts, joy, fears, anger and sorrow, not only of the individual but also of the group, and presenting these in melodic poems, composed with the rhythm of the *orak* dance at the back of the poet's mind. When the Acoli gather at the arena, they come to celebrate their loves and frustrations in love, or to lampoon those that would digress from the social paths. And it is the words of the poems that are exploited in the celebrations. Stung by the words of the poem, and moved by the rhythms of the drums and the half gourds, the dancer leaps in the air and moves his body according to the dance movements.

Being running commentaries on current affairs of the individual and the group, the songs of the *orak* dance soon become out of date and unfashionable; and new ones, equally transitory, are composed to replace them. It is in this aspect that these songs differ from the songs of the spirit possession dance, the chants at the ancestral shrine, the war songs and, to some extent, the dirges, which tend to last for very long periods of time.

The vast majority of the *orak* songs treat of local issues, and the jokes,

[7] E. E. Evans-Pritchard, *The position of women in savage societies*, London, 1965, p. 168. The essay entitled 'The dance' was first published in *Africa* in 1927.

the 'twist in the tail', are usually understood only by local people. A few of them, however, which are of exceptional beauty poetically and musically, become well known over wide areas, and may be in use for a comparatively long time. But as they travel from the original composer to other areas, other singers change the words and even the tune slightly to suit their own needs and circumstances. For example, if the original version of a love song praises the daughter of Wala-moi, the brown girl with a gap in her teeth, another version might praise the daughter of the chief, the black one. The act of singing is always a creative one. There are no fixed words or styles of singing a song, nor is the temper or pitch controlled. In short, there are no standard texts of any of the songs of the *orak* dance.

The Nanga[1]

This is by far the most important instrument of the Acoli people. It is a seven-stringed, boat-like, wooden[2] instrument. In most cases the poet musicians who play them make their own instruments. It is extremely versatile in that any song can be played on it: lullabies, war songs, love songs, satirical songs, dirges and even the songs that accompany the stories. No other musical instrument[3] can be compared to the *nanga* in this respect.

The instrument can be tuned in two keys: *ogodo*—major key for bright and gay songs, and *larumu*—minor key for grave and sad songs. The first three strings are collectively called *anyira*, girls, on account of their high pitches. String number six is the octave of string number one; and string number seven is the octave of string number two. String number four is called *orok*, poker, the one that pokes deeply, or *lakele*,[4] the one that brings out. String number five is called *labwami*, the arrogant one. For certain songs the labwami is not played on, and this is called *acura*. When all the strings are played on, this is called *agong*. It is these variations of the keys and styles of play that make the *nanga* so versatile.

There are only a few poet-musicians who play the *nanga* who are well known throughout Acoliland. Others are only known in their own localities. On the whole, the *nanga* players are not professional musicians. They live ordinary lives like other men, but are invited to social gatherings, especially those connected with marriage ceremonies.

Nanga players are loved and feared. Loved because of their ability to compose songs that touch the hearts of the people, whether they are

[1] Most of the information on this instrument was obtained from my friend the late Abonga Bongomin Lutwala, to whom I am most grateful.
[2] The strings are made from animal sinew, especially from the monkey. The wood is taken from the following trees: oywelo (vitex donaia); oyoro (*crateva adamsonii*); ananga lyec (*fiscus thonningii*); kibira or liira (*ziziphus abyssinica*); sambia (*markhaia platycalyx*); akwoo (*cordia abyssinica*) and oculuc, the Latin name of which is not known to me.
[3] The other stringed instruments are *adungu*, a three-stringed bow harp, played only by women; *lukembe*, played mainly by young men; and *opuk*, a five-stringed bow harp, played by men. In this chapter I am not concerned with the wind instruments.
[4] Note that the small drums in the *orak* dance are also called *lakele*.

songs of joy or of sorrow; feared because of their sharp tongues. They 'kill' people with their songs, as the following song suggests.

Lagama icito kwene?	*Where are you going, Lagama?*
Acito tung pa Too.	*I am going to Death's home.*
Cimot Too	*Take my greetings to Death.*
Iyoo!	*Okay!*
Ineno laco mo owero wer	*Listen, a certain man has composed a song,*
Wer neko Okoli.	*And the song has killed Okoli.*
Iyoo, iyoo, ndio,	*Yes, sure, sure.*
Apwoyo motti,	*Thank you for your greetings,*
Dong koni acimoto.	*I will take them to Death.*

In 1938 a blind poet from Lamogi was jailed by the colonial authorities. The chief of Lamogi, acting under the orders of the District Commissioner, had collected all able-bodied men from the area and taken them to Guly to work there under what was called the forced labour system. Adok Too responded to this challenge with the following song:

Cuna mito telo,	*My penis wants to get erect,*
An anongo min jago,	*When I find the sub-chief's mother,*
Agero benebene;	*I will fuck her all night long;*
Ee, cuna mito telle,	*Ee, my penis wants to get erect,*
An ayenyo min rwot,	*When I find the chief's mother*
Agero i dye yo;	*I will fuck her in the middle of the road;*
Ee, gira mito telo,	*Ee, my penis wants to get erect,*
An aito wi lela	*I am mounting the bicycle,*
Alaro Gulu;	*I am hurrying to Gulu;*
Ee, cuna mito telo,	*Ee, my penis wants to get erect,*
An anongo min Dici,	*When I find the District Commissioner's mother,*
Agero i bar Pece;	*I will fuck her in the football arena at Pece;*
Ee, cuna mito telo,	*Ee, my penis wants to get erect,*
An abedo i nge kwateng	*I will sit on the back of a kite,*
Watuk benebene;	*We shall fly all night;*
Ee, cuna mito telo,	*Ee, my penis wants to get erect,*
An anongo min king,	*When I find the king's mother,*
Jal, agero wi got.	*Man, I will fuck her on top of a hill.*

The blind poet, whose name is Omal Lakana, got himself another name when he was serving his two years' jail. It arose out of the following short poem:

Adok Too,	*If I could become Death,*
Adok Too,	*If I could become Death,*
Kono apoto i wi munu.	*I would fall on the white man.*

And today he is known by the name Adok Too.

Although today, young men are beginning to learn to play the *nanga*, in the past unmarried youths were prohibited from playing it. The story goes that a certain young man was hotly in love, but his father could not provide the bridewealth. He sat in his hut playing the *nanga* and singing about his love, and then hanged himself. From that time youths were not allowed to touch the instrument.

The *nanga* players are the main composers of music and poems in Acoliland. But other poets compose their songs using other instruments or none at all. The famous *nanga* players have a large repertoire of original compositions. They also learn other men's songs and transform them so that they sound almost original. Adok Too can play a whole night without repeating a single song, and often he composes new songs there and then. The new songs are quickly learnt by those present, who then distribute them throughout their locality, especially during the *orak* dances.

Otole—the war dance

The war songs which embody the history of a chiefdom are sung during the *otole* and *bwola* dances. As a result of the colonial experience, the chiefdoms have been more or less destroyed; but these dances are still performed, and indeed, they are now very popular. But the significance and meaning of these poems can best be understood in the context of the inter-chiefdom strifes, the wars with the Lango, who are referred to, contemptuously, as Omiro, the involvement of the Arab slave dealers and the British colonialists in Acoli politics.

In 1947 Wright, the District Commissioner of Acoli, ordered Eliya Aliker, chief of Payira, to construct a new road. Aliker, in turn, passed the order to the people of Labongo chiefdom, who had earlier been placed by the colonialists under the Payira chief. The people of Labongo refused, saying, 'What white ant ever eats across a stream?' Aliker went in person to Labongo to enforce the order and was met by the warriors of Labongo, who killed his bodyguard instantly. The chief shot and killed one man, and fled for his life. Led by a British officer called Wagstaff, the colonial mercenaries and the warriors of Payira attacked the Labongo, killed many people and took away their cattle as booty. The Labongo counter-attacked, killed many Payira warriors, and recaptured their cattle. A poet from Labongo sang the following song:

Aliker, kel dyangnga;	*Aliker, return my cattle;*
Ka ilwor,	*You coward,*
Mony Gala	*Tell the army of the white man*
Cung ikura,	*To stop, and wait for me,*
Waciwaromo Lamola.	*We shall meet at Lamola;*
Iyoo, iyoo,	*O yes, o yes;*
Muloji lwor,	*Muloji is a coward*
Dako loyo;	*Even a woman defeats him;*
Muloji lwor,	*Muloji is a coward*
Muloji lwor	*Muloji is a coward*
Dako loyo;	*Even a woman defeats him;*
Muloji lwor,	*Muloji is a coward,*
Ee, Agwe pyelo i kaki;	*Ee, he excretes in his khaki trousers;*
Aliker, kel dyangnga.	*Aliker, return my cattle.*

In 1886, the Arabs at Ajulu in Acoli killed Ywa Gimoro of Patiko chiefdom. One day, a convoy of Arabs was ambushed at Akworo, the crossing point on the Atiabar river. The slaughter was terrific. The following song records the victory:

Ee, mac ango ma wango Barara?	*Ee, what fire consumes Barara?*
Ililili, Ngaro, luyakara, i tugu;	*Listen to their wailings, Ngaro,*
Tonga romo i tugu,	*We win battle honours in the forest of barusus palms;*
Eyee, lililili, Ngaro;	*O, listen to their wailings, Ngaro;*
Nyikwara, i tugu;	*We win battle honours in the forest of barusus palms;*
Lamerok, lamerok,	*The enemy, the enemy,*
Luyakara, iyoo!	*We finished him, oh yes!*

In 1906 the Madi killed Abuga, chief of Atyak chiefdom. The warriors of Atyak retaliated and drove the Madi across the Nile. The following song celebrates the war:

Tonga ye,	*My spear, oh,*
Oweko Pagiri ongolo nam;	*It forced the Pagiri (Madi) to cross the river;*
Ee, aya, Adibaru,	*Ee, mother, Adibaru,*
Lamerok Adibaru,	*The enemy, Adibaru*
Lamerok, alimo,	*The enemy, I made him war captive,*
Ee, ineno kakare rac,	*Ee, look, the place was fearful;*
Jo Luwani.	*We are the people of Luwani.*

Even today these stirring poems still rouse feelings among former enemies. The football match between Acoli and Lango has always been very fiercely fought. The Acoli team and their supporters sing the following poem just before the start of the match:

Tong romo ki wedi ye,	*Spears met spears, oh;*
Ilamo lapii kwe,	*In vain you invoked your luck;*
Oboke olwedo,	*The leaves of the olwedo tree,*
Oboke olwedo mukonyi;	*It was the leaves of the olwedo tree that saved you;*
Lweny ma Ogwal Lameny ywa, ye,	*The battle that was led by Ogwal Lameny;*
Oweko Omiro owang i mac	*The Omiro were burnt in the fire*
Ame pura;	*Like kongonis;*

Ee, Omiro;	*Ee, Omiro,*
Oweko Omiro owang i mac	*The Omiro were burnt in the fire*
Ame pura;	*Like kongonis;*
Tong romo ki wedi ye.	*Spears met spears, oh.*

In 1909 Ogwal of Puranga chiefdom led his men and attacked a Lango village of Okole, the marshy area. The Acoli warriors had not studied the geography of the area and mistook the flat marshlands for dry land. The Lango, pretending to be fleeing, lured the Acoli men into the middle of the swamps and killed many of them. Encouraged by this victory, the Lango massed in great numbers and marched into Acoliland for a major raid. Their geography was equally weak, for they marched straight into a hunting ground. They were spotted, and the Acoli warriors surrounded them and set the dry grass ablaze. Many Langi were consumed by the fire and the spears of their adversaries.

In the traditional setting the *otole* dance was performed very rarely, usually once a year, during the dry season, when the crops had been harvested and stored. The organisational problems involved made it difficult to hold it more often. An *otole* dance session lasted many weeks or even months. A well-known proverb arose from such a situation. *Otole* dancers from Palabek stayed in Atyak till the end of the dry season; when the rains came, and the planting season had arrived, they still showed not the least intention of returning back to their homes in Palabek. The saying was, in effect, a request by the hosts that the visitors should go:

Bedo obedde,	*The visit is long enough,*
Atyak rac ku;	*Atyak are not bad;*
Oceke luweko kun molli.	*The sucking tube must be left*
	although it still flows with beer.

A visitor who has overstayed his welcome is often reminded of it by being told this short poem.

This is the largest, and, sociologically, perhaps the most interesting dance of the Acoli people. Men, women and youths of a clan, all armed as if for war: the men with spears and shields and huge headgear made of ostrich feathers, the women with battle-axes called *olayo*—'he (the enemy) has urinated'—form one dancing team, led by the clan head. The different clan teams together are commanded by the *rwot* chief of the chiefdom, who at the same time is also the head of the chiefly clan. The dance is exchanged between friendly chiefdoms.

Anywar has described the *otole* as the dance for wooing. And, as will be shown, many young men and women meet and woo each other during the session, but the *otole* is, primarily, a war dance. Platoons of brightly decorated and fully armed warriors, representing the different clans of the chiefdom, set out in single files. The chief's platoon marches in front. On reaching the village where the arena is situated there is regroupment, and the final preparation is made for the 'entry'. This is both spectacular and provocative. The entire army of dancers forms a solid block, the chief, women, girls and youths in the middle, and they then advance on the village in a mock attack.

The *oduru*, war alarm, is sounded, and the 'invaders', their spears unsheathed and shields at the ready, trot gently forward, destroying certain types of property on their way. Goats and sheep, calves and chickens are speared to death; as they go through unharvested simsim fields the entire crop is trodden underfoot; simsim stalks drying in the field are scattered and granaries riddled with spear holes. All this is supposedly done without malice and as a sign of friendship, and special care is taken to see that no human being is hurt. Toddlers caught playing in the swept compound, and old men and women unable to move quickly, are carefully avoided; houses are not touched.

Women of the village *goyo kijira*, yodel their welcome, and shout the *mwoc*, praise-name of their husbands' chiefdom. The men of the village blow their horns and trumpets and perform the *uc*, mock fight. They watch the destruction by the invaders with dignified restraint and calm, for the visitors are only paying back what they themselves did on their last visit.

On reaching the arena a large, roughly cleared circular ground, as big as a football pitch, the invaders stop. Drummers, three or four of them, escorted by an armed patrol of up to ten men, advance to take up their position at the drum post. This is an anxious moment, especially when another team is already performing. The patrol forces its way up to the drum post and stops the dance by *diyo min bul*, suppressing the mother drum. Stiff resistance is put up by the drum men around the post, who deliberately try to prevent the newcomers from reaching their objective. Often this sparks off a fight, and the organisers do their best to localise and extinguish an explosion.

The mother drum suppressed, those now occupying the arena

withdraw completely and move off in a body towards the stream, blowing their horns, while small groups break off to perform the *uc*. A well-known soloist from the visiting army calls out the first line of the chiefdom 'spear song', that is, the most stirring anthem of the chiefdom.

Tonga romo iya,	*I trust my spear,*
Maya lwor,	*Maya is cowardly,*
Orobo tua camo nyikwara	*Our young men earned battle honours*
Kom got.	*In the battle on the hill.*

The whole chiefdom army answers in a frightening and deafening

Ee, nyikwara, ee, ee	*Ee, battle honours, ee, ee,*
Soloist:	
Ayelu luneko,	*Ayelu is dead,*
Ee, nyikwara,	*Ee, battle honours,*
Chorus:	
Ayelu ye!	*Ayelu oh!*
Tonga romo iya!	*I trust my spear!*

As soon as the singing has started the drummers begin to play, giving a gentle trotting rhythm. The army of dancers now breaks up into the different clans, each led by the head of the clan, dancing a little distance ahead. Somewhere in the arena there is a scout who dances apart from the clan group and is followed by two women. This is the war leader of the group, and he maps out the direction to be followed by the main body.

In a few moments the entire arena looks like one confused mass because the different groups move in all directions, now stamping the ground in a stationary position, now prancing forwards, with shields held above the heads, now in a single file, and now in a solid block, etc. The situation is further confused by groups who break out of the main body to perform the *uc*, followed by their wives or girl-friends, who drive their axes into the ground, yodel and shout praises to the chiefdom of the men. Girls often fight among each other as they compete for a man.

The *uc* consists of confronting an 'enemy', real or imaginary, and attempting by clever manoeuvres to 'kill' him, without getting hurt oneself. When older men give lessons to youths they use sheathed spears, but the tip of the spear blade is left uncovered so that actual blood is let, as a lesson for the careless move.

Bere commented, 'This dance, though very spectacular on account of the very large number of armed men who take part in it, is not particularly beautiful, as it has no definite form and there is more shouting than singing.'[1] An Acoli would dismiss such comment with a shrug of the shoulder because, for him, there are few other more moving experiences. To begin with there is a basic underlying order, provided by the drummers and the singing. And, in the tense atmosphere of personal rivalries, inter-clan rivalries and interchiefdom jealousies, as well as friendship, the occasion lends itself to aggressive expressions of valour and temptations to settle old scores. The poems sung during the dance are expressions of the people of the chiefdom about the past glories of the chiefdom, its might, its victories and its future. There is no better occasion, no better atmosphere for the expression of chiefdom 'nationalism'.

After a number of songs have been danced to, lasting two to three hours, the dancers retire to the stream, clearing the arena for another dancing army. Later in the evening, while the older men continue to drink and discuss genealogies, past wars and other affairs, the youths hold the *lamoko-owang*, get-stuck dance, which continues all night long. As mentioned above, this visit lasts weeks and even months. The friendship that is established between members of different chiefdoms is strengthened by the marriages that take place between the young people. This friendship is exploited during times of crisis, such as when one of the chiefdoms is attacked, or wishes to attack another chiefdom. It is the chiefdoms between whom the *otole* dances are exchanged that normally act as allies.

It is interesting to note that not all the chiefdoms of Acoli performed this dance. Indeed, the dance seems to have been confined to the Padibe, Palabek, Palaro, Payira and Atyak. The chiefdoms to the east such as Paimol, Lira Pa-luo, Puranga and Bwobo, excel in the *bwola* dance. Some chiefdoms, such as Lamogi, seem not to have evolved either of the dances, but are famous for their performance of the *orak*, and their poets are famous throughout Acoliland for their bitter tongues.

The *bwola* dance differs from the *otole* in a number of ways, although the poems sung during the dance are similar to those sung at the *otole* dance, in that they are also historical. It is usually danced at the chief's enclosure; hence its name, the chief's dance. But it may also be performed in another place, such as the home of the clan head, or at the

[1] Op. cit.

funeral of a war leader, *oteka*. The normal occasions for the performance of the *bwola* are: the installation and burial of a chief; during the building of the ancestral shrine at the chief's homestead; at the celebrations for the opening of a new settlement during rain-making ceremonies; and when sacrifices are made at the chiefdom shrine. In short, the *bwola* is performed on what we may call 'state' occasions, when the interest of the chiefdom as a whole is involved.

Unlike the *otole* with its aggressive show and much running about, the *bwola* is entirely peaceful and most sophisticated. Nobody carries any weapon. The men are armed with small drums and drumsticks, and the women carry flywhisks made from giraffe tails. There are five main movements: *poto*, the entry into the arena: all the dancers form up in a column four deep, and dance into the arena. The second movement is called *ayara*, when the column is made into a circle. *Agoya* is the next movement, when a number of songs are danced to. This is the main part of the dance. It is followed by the *labala*, in which the men put their drums on the ground and demonstrate their skills in complicated body movements. The last movement is the exit, when the circle becomes a column once more, and the dancers leave the arena.

Each *bwola* song has its own steps and body movements, as well as its own drumming. In other words, in learning a new *bwola* song, one is at the same time learning a new dance. The most impressive thing about the *bwola* dance is the simultaneity with which all the dancers hit their small drums and move their bodies, as they dance to the measured rhythms of the *min acel*, the mother drum. This symbolises perfect unity and harmony within the chiefdom. During the performance of the dance, mothers put their male babies under the *min acel* for brief periods. Far from frightening the babies, it is believed that the beautiful rhythm of the dance sinks into the baby at this age and, when he grows up, he takes to the dance naturally.

Funeral Rites and Dance

The dirges of Acoli form an important part of the conventionalised and dramatised outburst of grief and wailing, with which the people face the supreme crisis of life-death. When a man is critically ill his father or elder brother or son is called to his deathbed to hear his last wishes. Soon after death has occurred the women begin wailing. The men begin to dig the grave while some of them, in tears, blow their horns and stage the *uc*, mock fight. Messages are sent out to relatives, and soon a crowd is assembled at the homestead where death has struck.

When the grave is ready, a brief ceremony, *kwer*, takes place inside the house where the corpse is lying. It is attended only by a few elderly people. The ritual differs in detail from area to area. The following is what happens among the Payira. The widow is made to lie over the dead man, and she embraces him. The father of the dead man, or his eldest son, covers the couple with a duiker skin and taps their heads with *olutu kwon* (a wooden spoon used for making millet bread), and *ogwec* (a wooden spoon used for making gravy). Then the head of the dead man is shaved and smeared with *pala*, red ochre and oil. A piece of string is tied around the chest of the widow and another round her head, and the leaves of the *olwedo* tree are hung on the strings. This is called *tweyo cola*, tying sorrows on the body. Her head is then covered with the duiker skin, and she is led off into the wilderness, where she stays until the burial is over. In the same way a husband does not attend the actual burial of his wife.

The corpse is laid on its side, in the grave with the head resting on a head-rest. All present gather around and throw handfuls of soil into the grave. The pit is then filled in, and a mound made. A goat is slaughtered and roasted on an open fire, and distributed and eaten mostly by the people who buried the dead man.

Three or four days later, the second stage of the mourning is marked by a ceremony called *puyu lyel*, smearing the grave. The immediate area of the grave is tidied up and smeared with a black clayey soil. This is usually a local affair, attended only by the people of the homestead.

The final ceremony, called *guru lyel*, takes place at a carefully chosen time to ensure maximum attendance. Many months usually elapse between death and this feast. Its size depends on the socio-economic status of the dead person. It is not held for children and youths. And, as Shakespeare put it, 'when beggars die, there are no comets seen; the heavens themselves blaze forth the death of princes'. In July 1962 the *guru lyel* of Adwany, widow of Okelo, took place in Gulu. She had died at a ripe old age, and because of this, it would be expected that many people would come to the occasion; but there were only eighteen people. A dirge that was repeated several times was a fitting commentary on this particular situation:

Omera lwenyo ki atero biri,	*My brother fights with barbed-headed arrows,*
Lwenyo bongo omin,	*He fights alone,*
Omera lakony kore peke,	*There is no brother beside him;*
Tin oweko paco	*Today he has left the homestead*
Odong ma lik;	*And it is fearful,*
Awobi lakong kore peke,	*The youth fights alone;*
Bedo onyo kibedo kenikeni.	*Today, men live alone, no brother beside him,*
Omera lwenyo ki bur.	*My brother fights with the grave.*

Compare this with the *guru lyel* of Rwot Awic of Payira in 1946. All the clan heads of Payira chiefdom were there, and all the chiefs of Acoliland went. The Mukama of Bunyoro was represented by his own brother and the keeper of the Palace. Hundreds of goats and cattle were slaughtered, and the feast lasted many weeks.

On the morning of the appointed day the widow is led off into the wilderness once more, and her head is shaved. The strings of sorrow around her head and chest are untied; hence the name of the ceremony, *gonyo cola*, untying sorrows from the body. Everybody in the homestead is shaved and this marks the end of mourning. Later, during the day, groups of relatives and their wives begin to arrive, bringing cattle and goats and material for making beer.

About fifty or so yards from the homestead the mourners, who up to now were in a single file, form up in battle formation and storm the homestead in a mock attack. The women running behind them, armed with battle-axes, make ululations and shout the praise-name of the clan. On regrouping, the soloist leaps up and stamps the ground rhythmically singing the first line of the dirge, the rest take up the chorus, as follows:

Soloist

Yee, mac owang Layima ye,	*Oh, fire rages at Layima, oh,*
Mac owang kulu Cumu.	*Fire rages in the valley of river Cumu.*

Chorus

Owang nginyinginyi woko;	*Everything is utterly utterly destroyed;*
Kono ao pa min to;	*If I could reach the homestead of death's mother,*

Soloist

Nyara kono ariyo raa ma bor;	*My daughter, I would make a long grass torch;*

Chorus

Kono ao pa min to,	*If I could reach the homestead of death's mother,*
Kono awango nginyinginyi woko;	*I would destroy everything utterly utterly;*
Mac owang kulu Cumu ye!	*Like the fire that rages in the valley of river Cumu, oh!*

The dancing is accompanied by drumming and the scrubbing of large half-gourds on planks of wood. The dancers may dance three to five songs before another group replaces them. Later on in the night there are joint sessions. As in all other Acoli dances there is much competition, not only between individuals, but also between the various groups taking part in the *guru lyel*. There is ample scope for self-display in the costumes, singing, performing the mock fight and so on. There is room for both individual exhibition and group performance.

The system of inheritance allows the widow considerable freedom in the choice of the inheritor, *lalaku*. The ceremony of *yokko pala*, also called *ciddo pala*, removing the mourning ochre, takes place three or four months after the *guru lyel*. At this ceremony the widow is introduced to her new husband in the presence of the elders. During the period between the death of the husband and this ceremony, the widow indicates who among the dead man's brothers should be the guardian of her children. Apart from other economic considerations, to be thus chosen is a vote of confidence; it is also a big step up in the social order. It is the jealousy this causes among clansmen that produces the dirges which are an attack on the living.

The following love song, sung during the night joint sessions, is aimed at the young widows:

Gin pa maa,	*Beloved of my mother-in-law,*
Acel long;	*The only one of her mother;*
Lapaka Olwa mito meye do.	*Lapaka Olwa seeks her lover, oh.*
Laberri kono atimo ning?	*The beautiful one, how can I get her?*
Okwero co gu ducu ba;	*She has rejected all other men;*
Anyaka mito meye;	*She seeks only her lover;*
Gin pa maa,	*Beloved of my mother-in-law*
Macalo kwac ni	*Is like a leopard;*
Anyaka mito meye.	*The young woman seeks her lover.*

The general atmosphere during the dance is determined by the age of the dead person. It is restrained and sad if it is the funeral dance of a man struck down at the peak of his manhood, say, about thirty to fifty years of age. You may hear occasional wailing of the women mingling with the drumming, the singing and the scrubbing of the half-gourds. The nearest relatives dance with tears on their cheeks. It may be said that the dirges have their fullest meaning and significance when sung for such a person.

At the funeral of an old person the situation is very different. Before the death of such a person *ma nyime cok*, whose end is near, women in the homestead joke with him or her, and ask, 'Granny, when will you die so that we may enjoy a dance?' and some of them even make preparations publicly for the occasion. Small children play with him or her like a doll. They give him earth instead of bread and laugh as the old one puts the earthen lump in his toothless mouth. On announcing the death of such a person women pretend to weep, but complain that it is difficult to shed tears. So that although the same dirges are sung at the funeral dance of the very old, they do not seem to carry the same significance and meaning. There is no tragedy in the death of such people, and at night there is much sexual activity. It is said the dead must be born again, and children conceived at such funerals are named after the grand old man or woman.

PART II

Children's Songs

Golden slumbers kiss your eyes,
Smiles awake you when you rise,
Sleep pretty darling, do not cry,
And I will sing a lullaby.
                    Thomas Dekker : Lullaby from *Patient Grissill*

Min latin tedo dyewor

Min latin do,
Tedo dyewor;
Min latinwa ni,
Tedo dyewor;
Oneno dek ocek,
Kella gira,
Gwok iturra kore;

Oneno dek pudi yo,

Ter latin ka tuku tunu.

Baby's mother cooks at night

Baby's mother oh,
She cooks at night;
Our baby's mother,
Cooks at night;
When she sees the food is ready,
She shouts, bring my baby to me,
Do not let him fall and break his
back;
But when the food is not yet ready,
oh,
She says, please take the baby to play
awhile.

Latin kok ngo?	*Why does the baby cry?*
Latin kok ngo?	*Why does the baby cry?*
Kome rem bo?	*Is he ill?*
Onyur ling ling,	*Baby, stop crying,*
Lapidi meri peke;	*Your nurse is not here;*
In ka ikok ango?	*Why do you cry oh,*
Lapidi meri peke;	*Is it because your nurse is not here?*
Nyurri ling ba,	*Baby, stop crying oh,*
Lapidi meri obeno;	*Let the strap be your nurse;*
Latin kok ngo?	*Why does the baby cry?*
Meru otedo aluru ki kwon;	*Your mother has cooked quails and millet bread;*
Onyur ling ling,	*Baby, stop crying, oh,*
Meni ocelo aluru ki kwon.	*Your mother has fried quails and millet bread.*

3
Kitino kany dega

Kitino kany dega,
An lakolo;
Kitino kany dega,
An lakolo;
Onongo maa ocito i kulu,
An lakolo;
Onongo maa ocito ka yen,

An lakolo;
Onongo maa ocito ka doo,

An lakolo;
Kitino kany dega,
An lakolo.

Children in this home do not like me

Children in this home do not like me,
I like fighting;
Children in this home do not like me,
I like fighting;
When my mother goes to the well,
I like fighting;
When my mother goes to collect firewood,
I like fighting;
When my mother goes to weed the garden,
I like fighting;
Children in this home do not like me,
I like fighting.

4

Luduku pa Langalanga

Luduku pa Langalanga
Anga mucelo?
Wacelo, wacelo, wacelo, baa yaa!

Luduku pa Langalanga
Anga mucelo?
Wacelo, wacelo, wacelo, baa yaa!

Baa-likali-taya,
Litaya;
Baa-likali-taya,
Litaya.

The guns of Langalanga

The guns of Langalanga
Who fires them?
We fire them, we fire them, we fire
  them, bang, bang;

The guns of Langalanga
Who fires them?
We fire them, we fire them, we fire
  them, bang, bang;

Bang, bang, bang, bang,
Big bang;
Bang, bang, bang, bang,
Big bang.

5
Dini-dini ye

Dini-dini ye,	*I hit you hard, I hit you hard, oh*
Otoo ber;	*I hit you hard, I hit you hard, oh,*
Dani ma yam otoo te layata,	*It is good that she died;*
	Your grandmother who died among the potato-heaps,
Otoo ber;	*It is good that she died;*
Dini-dini ye,	*I hit you hard, I hit you hard, oh,*
Otoo ber,	*It is good that she died;*
Dani ma yam otoo te laywee,	*Your grandmother who died under the broom bushes,*
Otoo ber;	*It is good that she died;*
Lamanya-manya puk!	*I close your eyes completely.*

6

Okutu oryang	*Thorns of the oryang tree*
Okutu oryang	*Thorns of the oryang tree*
Ma kititino,	*Are small and sharp;*
Okutu oryang,	*Thorns of the oryang tree*
Lakalagwec;	*Are fast like the lakalagwec bird;*
Okutu oryang	*Thorns of the oryang tree*
Ma kititino,	*Are small and sharp;*
Okutu oryang,	*Thorns of the oryang tree*
Lakalagwec;	*Are fast like the lakalagwec bird;*
Cub, iyiki,	*Let it penetrate and leave it there,*
Cubu tryak,	*It makes a small blast;*
Lakalagwec;	*It is fast like the lakalagwec bird*
Cub, iyiki,	*Let it penetrate and leave it there,*
Cubu tryak,	*It makes a small blast;*
Lakalagwec.	*It is fast like the lakalagwec bird.*

7
Cieng, cieng, tipo oyeto meni

Cieng, cieng,
   tipo oyeto meni;
Cieng, cieng,
   tipo oyeto meni.

Tipo, tipo,
   cieng oyeto meni;
Tipo, tipo,
   cieng oyeto meni.

*Sun, sun, shadow has insulted
your mother*

*Sun, sun, shadow has insulted your
mother;*
*Sun, sun, shadow has insulted your
mother.*

*Shadow, shadow, sun has insulted
your mother;*
*Shadow, shadow, sun has insulted
your mother.*

8
Lililili Lango obino

Lililili Lango obino,
Lili ye;
Lililili Lango obino,
Lili ye;
Tum pa nera kok kuca,

Lili ye;
Bila pa wora kok kuca,

Lili ye;
Tum pa omera kok kuca,

Lili ye;
Lililili Lango obino,
Lili ye;
Lililic.

Lililili the Lango are coming

Lililili the Lango are coming,
Lili oh ;
Lililili the Lango are coming,
Lili oh ;
The trumpet of my uncle sounds that
  way,
Lili oh ;
The horn of my father sounds that
  way,
Lili oh ;
The trumpet of my brother sounds
  that way,
Lili oh ;
Lililili the Lango are coming,
Lili oh ;
Lililic.

33

9

Okwata dong obino

Okwata dong obino,
Piny odoko oro;
Kwateng mubino,
Piny odoko oro.

The kites have come

The kites have come,
The dry season is here;
The coming of the kites means
The dry season is here.

10

Min latin	Baby's mother

Min latin

Min latin ocito kulu,
Onongo lwango opong te
    latin bic.

Baby's mother

Baby's mother went to the well,
She found baby's anus full of flies.

11

Awiyo tolla	*I make my own strings*
Awiyo tolla do,	*I make my own strings,*
Awiyo tolla do,	*I make my own strings,*
Wi laaro;	*On the rocks;*
Awiyo tolla do,	*I make my own strings,*
Awiyo tolla do,	*I make my own strings,*
Wi laaro;	*On the rocks;*
Tol ma kiwiyo ma kititino,	*The strings I make are only small ones,*
Bwolle kwede, bwolle kwede;	*I play with them, I play with them;*
Ogwal goyo bul,	*Ogwal beats the drum,*
An agoyo ni kiling,	*I also beat the drum, it goes kiling,*
Kiling, kiling, ki loka ca,	*Kiling, kiling, on the other side of the stream,*
Jo Labongo goyo oduru;	*And the people of Labongo raise an alarm;*
Kiling, eno ba!	*Kiling, listen!*
Naka ceng abin ki tua kuca,	*Once I came from our home over there,*
Keto cunya kom cii omera ye,	*I fell in love with my brother's wife,*
Kom cii omera ye,	*With my brother's wife,*
Kom gin pa ji.	*I wanted other people's things.*

12

Kidwe, kidwe, kidwe

Kidwe, kidwe, kidwe,
Meni ocito kwene?
Maa ocito kulu.
Kulu ne nga?
Kulu Lacele.
Celu wiyo tol,
Wicce ye, wicce ye,

Me dyang, me dyang;
Celu pa Malakwang,
Malakwang otingo dyang
Tero Pailoto.
Ceng ma anongo Alum,
Bipoto twengel!

Child, child, child

Child, child, child,
Where has your mother gone?
My Mother has gone to the well.
The well, what is its name?
The well called Lacele.
Celu is making a rope,
*The rope is being made, is being
   made*

For a cow, for a cow.
Celu is son of Malakwang,
Malakwang is taking a cow
To Pailoto.
The day I meet Alum,
I will throw her down at once!

13
Acel, aryo, ni tidi mo

Acel, aryo, ni tidi mo;
Wanni, wanni Liboro;
Kitino moni, gin aryo kenyo;
Obolo tyene nge gang;

Ee, mabure do:
Onongo mac man wang Palabek;

Tin adok kwene?
Idiyo duda do;
Onongo cun cwari
Kiboko onini!

One, two, she says, it is too small

One, two, she says, it is too small;
I, I and Liboro;
Little ones, two little kids;
She threw her legs open behind the house;

Ee, she said, it is useless;
There was this fire burning at Palabek;

She said, where shall I go today?
You are pressing my buttocks, oh;
Your husband's penis
Is a hippopotamus hide whip!

The Love Song

> I waited for him everywhere, alarmed.
> I scanned the road to Aulis day and night:
> My heart in search of him flew far ahead
> Seeking Achilles's face in everything.
> Racine: Iphigenia

> By night on my bed I sought him whom my soul loveth:
> I sought him, but found him not . . .
> Behold, though art fair, my love . . .
> Thy teeth are like a flock of sheep that are even shorn,
> which came up from the washing . . .
> Thy breasts are like two young roes that are twins,
> which feed among the lilies.
> The Song of Solomon

> Why are your breasts prettier than the breasts of other girls?
> Your chest and your legs are as clear as ivory,
> Your back is flexible, your eyes are bright,
> How pretty you are . . .
> Indo-China: Hola pretty girl

14
Larema okutu kany?

Larema okutu kany?
Okutu bila ma lungeyo.
Orobo tua,
Uwinyo bila pa meya?

Bor piny bala ba!
Bor piny ki liwota.

Lutino tua,
Uwinyo bila pa meya?

Can dyang balo mere!

Can dyang pa liwota.
Awobe tua,
Winyu bila pa meya.

Liwota okutu kany?
Okutu bula ma lungeyo weng.
Orobo tua,
Winyu bila pa meya.

Where has my love blown his horn?

Where has my love blown his horn?
The tune of his horn is well known.
Young men of my clan,
Have you heard the horn of my love?

The long distance has ruined me, oh!
The distance between me and my companion.

Youths of my clan,
Have you heard the horn of my love?

The shortage of cattle has ruined my man!

The poverty of my love.
You men of my clan,
Listen to the horn of my love.

Where has my love blown his horn?
The tune of his horn is well known.
Young men of my clan.
Listen to the horn of my clan.

Leng wange ka aneno

Leng wange ka aneno,

Abolo kwon piny;
Oh, lamin apwai we,
Leng wang meya.

Otono ngute, ka aneno,
Anino ku kwak;
Oh, latin pa mara,

Ngute bol toro.

Kedo pyere ka abongo,
Ato woko;
Oh, lamin apwai we,
Kedo pyer meya.

Kere pa mere ka aneno,

Lake nyim kila;

Oh, latin pa wora;

Kere lak meya.

Nya pa twon balo wiya,

Anyomo olo twal;
Ada, lamin apwai we!
Yom pyer meya.

When I see the beauty on my beloved's face

When I see the beauty on my beloved's face,
I throw away the food in my hand;
Oh, sister of the young man, listen;
The beauty on my beloved's face.

Her neck is long, when I see it
I cannot sleep one wink;
Oh, the daughter of my mother-in-law,
Her neck is like the shaft of the spear.

When I touch the tattoos on her back,
I die;
Oh, sister of the young man, listen;
The tattoos on my beloved's back.

When I see the gap in my beloved's teeth,
Her teeth are white like dry season simsim;
Oh, daughter of my father-in-law listen,
The gap in my beloved's teeth.

The daughter of the bull confuses my head,
I have to marry her;
True, sister of the young man, listen;
The suppleness of my beloved's waist.

Okwanyo ger Lumule

She has taken the path to Nimule

Okwanyo ger lumule;
Diki dwogo.
Woto muturu adyany.

She has taken the path to Nimule;
She will return tomorrow.
As she walked away her buttocks danced.

Kel Alyeka anen.
O!, laber orii i tim.

Bring Alyeka, let me see her.
Oh, the beautiful one has stayed away long.

Wanga rii ki iyo;
Wanga ki yo,
Omera, kel Alyeka anen.

My eyes are fixed on the path;
My eyes on the path,
Brother, bring Alyeka, let me see her;

Rwot mon,
Alyeka, nyal ma lano.

Chief of all women,
Alyeka, the brown one.

Okwanyo gudu pa Otara,
Koni oo.
Myero ki rwot awobi.
Kel Alyeka anen ba!
O!, laber obutu i tim.

She took the white man's road,
She will arrive just now.
She is fit for the chief of youths.
Bring Alyeka, let me see her please!
Oh, the beautiful one has spent a night away.

Wanga rii ki iyo;
Wanga ki yo,
Kabaka, kel meya anen,
Alyeka, anyaka koni oo.

My eyes are fixed on the road,
My eyes on the road,
Kabaka, bring Alyeka, let me see her,
Alyeka, she will soon be here.

Okwanyo ger ma piny,
Wanga ki yo;
Akuru ki yutu piny;
Omera, kel Alyeka anen.
O!, opor Palabek.
Wanga rii ki iyo,
Wanga ki yo,
Omera, kel Alyeka bota ba,

She took the lower path,
My eyes are on the path;
I will wait for her at sunset;
Brother, bring Alyeka, let me see her.
Oh, she has eloped at Palabek.
My eyes are fixed on the path,
My eyes on the path,
Brother, bring Alyeka, let me see her please.

Alyeka: anyaka nyal ma lano.

Alyeka, the brown girl.

Nya pa Lekamoi

Ai maa,
Ineno nya pa Lekamoi
Mudongo nyen.
Nyako dwogo awene ka?
Meya bino awene?
Nya pa twon,
Dako bi aneni, nye;
Nya pa Lekamoi,
Lawi anyira,
Gira oo awene?
Oh, Abul ma rwot mon.

Otono ngute calo twol abino,

Ineno nya pa Lekamoi,
Lakere,
Lake poro buru.
Oh, mere dwogo awene?
Nya pa twon
Abul, kel teke, nye.

Nya pa Lekamoi,
Mudongo nyen,
Dano mito weng,
Oh, Abul ma rwot mon.

Anyaka coro ki yo Anaka,

Ineno nya pa Lekamoi,
Odongo lunede,
Iporo ki nya pa anga?

Liwota dwogo awene?
Nya pa twon,
Dako bi awari, nye.

Nya pa Lekamoi,
Lawi anyira,
Cuka awobe mito, ba,

Abul ma rwot mon.

Daughter of Lekamoi

Oh, mother,
Behold the daughter of Lekamoi
Who has just grown up.
Young woman, when will she return?
When does my love come back?
Daughter of the bull,
Woman, come, let me see you, listen;
Daughter of Lekamoi,
Leader of the girls,
When does my own arrive?
Oh, Abul, chief of women.

Her neck resembles a snake
coming out of a vase,

Behold, daughter of Lekamoi,
The gap in her teeth,
Her teeth are like ash.
Oh, when does my love come back?
Daughter of the bull,
Abul, come and dance before me,
listen.

Daughter of Lekamoi
Who has just shot up,
All the men want her,
Ah, Abul, chief of women.

My girl appears on the path from
Anaka,

Behold the daughter of Lekamoi,
Tall, graceful,
With whose daughter can you
compare her?

My companion, when will she return?
Daughter of the bull,
Woman, come, I will take you from
your husband, listen.

Daughter of Lekamoi,
Leader of the girls,
Yes, all the men are in love with her,
oh,
Abul, chief of women.

Tidi pa liwota

Tidi pa liwota ye,
Tidi ma myero, ada;
Tidi,
Liwota yo,
Tidi,
Liwota dong mot,

Layaa na.

My beloved is small

My beloved is small, oh,
She is small and truly beautiful;
She is small,
My love, oh,
She is small,
*Grow up slowly my love, there is no
    hurry,*
Oh my love.

Liwota bwola ki doge

*My companion deceives me
with words of her mouth*

Tidi, liwota bwola

*She is small, my companion deceives
me*

Ki doge do;
Aba, oloko lok tino;
Okedo pyere,
Bwola nono,
Aba, oloko lok tino;
Tidi, layaa bita nono,

With words from her mouth;
Father, she talks like a child;
She has cut tattoos on her back,
But she is merely deceiving me,
Father, she talks like a child.
*She is small, my love is only teasing
me,*

Latin otimo lok mingo;
Obwonyo ca, bita nono,

The child does silly things;
*Look, she smiles, but is only teasing
me,*

Aba, oloko lok tino.

Father, she speaks like a child.

Lek tin obwola

Kitinne, lek tin obwolo an,

Lek man lanywar;
Kitinne, lek tin ocabo an,

Lek man labwoc;
Kitinne, jonni tin aleko meya,

Lek man lakolo;
O!, jonni lek man obwola ye,

Lek man lanywar;
Kitinne, jonni tin abutu ki meya,

Lek man lakolo;
Kitinne, aco abongo obaya, mwa;

Lek man lakolo;
Ada, kitinne, lek tin anywara ba,

Lek man labwoc;
Kitinne, anongo adyako obaya,

Lek man lakolo;
Jonni, lek tin otima rac,

Lek man labwoc.

A dream deceived me today

My age-mates, a dream deceived me today,

What a naughty dream;
My age-mates, a dream made me a fool today,

What an insulting dream;
My age-mates, people, today I dreamed of my love,

What a cruel dream;
Oh, people, a dream deceived me today, ee,

What a naughty dream;
My age-mates, people, today I slept with my love,

What a cruel dream;
My age-mates, I woke up and felt all over the sleeping mat, all in vain;

What a cruel dream;
Truly, my age-mates, today a dream deceived me, ee,

What an insulting dream;
My age-mates, I found the sleeping mat wet;

What a cruel dream;
My people, a dream treated me badly today,

What a naughty dream.

Lim odoko peke

Lim odoko peke,
An ce anongo dyang kwene
Me lakel meya?
    Laber, cung,
    Awari ye!

Lamera mo pe, nye,
Agaro dyang kanye
Akel ki cega?
    Laber, cung,
    Awari ye!

Lim otimo rac, ye,

Akwalo dyang pa anga
Anyom ki dako?
    Lakere, cung,

    Awari ye!

Wora bene peke,
Latinni nongo lim kwene

Me lacul luk?

    In, cung,
    Awari ye!

Lim odoko peke, nye,
Lim kor lakeya,

Akel ki Kele;
    Laber, cung,
    Awari ye!

The bridewealth is not there

The bridewealth is not there,
Where shall I find the cattle
With which to bring my love home?
    Beautiful one, stop, wait for me,
    Let me take you even from your
      husband!

And I have no sister, listen,
Where shall I gather the cattle
With which to bring my wife home?
    Beautiful one, stop, wait for me,
    Let me take you even from your
      husband!

Shortage of wealth has treated me
    cruelly, oh,
Whose cattle shall I steal,
So that I may marry my woman?
    You with the gap in your teeth,
      stop, wait for me,
    Let me take you even from your
      husband!

And I have no father,
Where will this young man find
    money
With which to pay the fornication
    fine?
    You, stop, wait for me,
    Let me take you even from your
      husband!

The bridewealth is not there, listen,
I will use the bridewealth of my
    uncle's daughter
To bring Kele home;
    Beautiful one, stop, wait for me,
    Let me take you even from your
      husband!

Wora kel lim	*Father, bring the bridewealth*

Wora kel lim,
Akel ki dako na;
Cwinya cwer,
Cwinya wang pire,
Lapal cwinya do;
Nyodo pa min Owiny,
Cero wanga nino.

Lapal cwinya,
Ngat ma gudu meya,
Lut-kot goyo woko,
Wi-yo, cwinya wang pire,
Lamo tino,
Nyodo pa min Owiny
Cero wanga nino.

Lapal cwinya ney,
Ngat ma gudu meya,
Twol kong temo twal,
Wi-yo, iya ton pire,
Lamo tino do,
Nyodo pa min Owiny
Cero wanga nino!

Lamo tino,
Wora ka ato
An aceni woko,

Wi-yo, wi-yo;
Lapal cwinya nye,
Nyodo pa min Owiny
Balo wiya ye;

Lamo tino,
Ngat ma gudu meja,
Pig wanga cwer remo;
Cwinya cwer,
Cwinya wang pire,
Lapal cwinya, nye,
Nyodo pa min Owiny
Cero wanga nino.

Father, bring the bridewealth,
Let me bring my love home;
I am sad,
My heart is on fire for her;
The woman of my bosom, oh,
Born of the mother of Owiny,
Keeps my eyes from sleep.

Woman of my bosom,
If anybody touches my beloved,
He will be struck by lightning,
Oh, oh, my heart is on fire for her,
Oil of my youth,
Born of the mother of Owiny,
Keeps my eyes from sleep.

Woman of my bosom, listen,
If anybody touches my beloved,
He will be struck by a snake;
Oh, my heart bleeds for her;
Oil of my youth,
Born of the mother of Owiny,
Keeps my eyes from sleep.

Oil of my youth,
Father, should I die
I shall become a fierce vengeance
  ghost and kill you:
Oh, oh,
Woman of my bosom,
Born of the mother of Owiny,
Confuses my head.

Oil of my youth,
If anybody touches my beloved,
I shall shed tears of blood;
My heart bleeds,
My heart is on fire for her,
Woman of my bosom, listen,
Born of the mother of Owiny
Keeps my eyes from sleep.

23

Duka pa wang	*The eye shop*
Duka pa wang	*The shop where they sell eyes,*
Tye kwene?	*Where is it?*
Larema kono aneno awene?	*When shall I ever see my beloved?*
Akoro laber ki kiniga.	*I praise the beautiful one with anger.*

24

Tum pa larema

Tum pa larema
Tum oyoro;
Awinyo
Onyo koma koyo.

My beloved's trumpet

My beloved's trumpet
Is made from oyoro tree;
When I hear its tune
I shiver as if with cold.

25

Aba, ka iming

Nyako
Ee, aba, ka iming
Lutera nono.

Laco
Nya pa rwot
Cal ki winyo nam.

Nyako
Lalwak omera,
Wato kwedi,
Larok omera,
Loko lok dano.

Laco
Ka lok odoko rac
Wapor woko apora.

Nyako
Aba, laracci
Bwoli nono.

Laco
Nya pa rwot otuc i bar,

Cal ki jo apar;
Nya pa rwot cal ki owalu.

Nyako
I bar Pece kuka
Wamyelo kwedi atena;

Lalwak omera,
Iloko lok dano ba.

Laco
Ka lok odoko rac
Kilwenyo woko alwenya;
Laracci amayo dakone woko
Oted ki cinge.

Father, if you are stupid

Girl
Father, if you are stupid,
They will take me without paying the
* bridewealth.*

Man
The daughter of the chief
Is like a lake bird.

Girl
Age-mate of my brother,
We shall die together.
Friend of my brother
Has spoken the truth.

Man
If the matter becomes bad
I shall elope with you.

Girl
Father, the ugly man
Deceives you.

Man
When the daughter of the chief enters
* the arena,*
She is like ten people;
The daughter of the chief is like the
* crested crane.*

Girl
In the arena at Pece
We shall dance close together and
* touch each other;*
Age-mate of my brother,
You have spoken the truth, oh.

Man
If the matter becomes bad
We shall fight it out;
I will take the ugly man's wife,
Let him cook with his own hands.

51

Nyako	Girl
Larok omera	*Friend of my brother*
Iloko lok dano do;	*You have spoken the truth;*
Aba, tulekeni tera ku.	*Father, the rough-skinned man will never take me.*
Ka lok odoko rac	*If the matter becomes bad,*
Wakwalle woko akwala.	*We shall slip away, secretly.*
Laco	Man
Nya pa twon	*Daughter of the bull*
Cal ki owalu.	*Is like the crested crane.*
Nyako	Girl
Aba, larac-okang	*Father, the ugly and barren man,*
Ce gudu bad anga?	*Whose hand will he touch?*
Aba, ka iming,	*Father, if you are stupid*
Lutera nono.	*They will take me without paying the bridewealth.*
Laco	Man
Nya pa rwot	*When the daughter of the chief*
Ocoro i bar,	*Storms into the arena,*
Rom ki nya pa anga?	*With whose daughter can you compare her?*
Nyako	Girl
Lalwak omera,	*Age-mate of my brother,*
Iloko lok dano do.	*You have spoken the truth, oh!*
Laco	Man
Nya pa twon obunyu,	*When the daughter of the bull smiles,*
Lake nyim kila.	*Her teeth are like dry simsim.*
Nyako	Girl
Layaana	*My love,*
Iloko lok dano ya.	*You have spoken the truth, oh!*
Laco	Man
Nya pa twon, meya,	*Daughter of the bull, my love,*
Wato kwedi acel.	*We shall die together.*

Nyako
Lalwak omera
Iloko lok dano;
Wora, in,
Laracci lubu kor anga?
Layaana okwilo lok

Cubu iya.

Laco
Ee, nya pa twon
Poro rii.

Nyako
Meca, ka ojwato aula

Balo wiya;

Laco
Lamin apwai,
Iloko lok dano ba.

Nyako
Rwot awobe ocoro i bar,

Cal ki apoli mungok;

Larema ocoro idibu

Calo ngu.
Aba, lagoroni tera kwene?

Laco
Larema,
Iloko lok dano.

Girl
Age-mate of my brother,
You have spoken the truth;
Father, listen,
This ugly man, whom does he follow?
When my beloved whispers into my
    ears,
His words spear deep into my inside.

Man
Ee, the daughter of the bull
Is like the giraffe.

Girl
When my beloved swishes his
    arm-swish,
My head gets confused;

Man
Sister of my friend
You have spoken the truth, oh.

Girl
When the chief of youths enters the
    arena,
He is like a water-buck breaking the
    circle of hunters;
When my friend enters into the
    arena
He is like a lion.
Father, where can this weak old man
    take me?

Man
My love,
You have spoken the truth.

26

Kel kweyo

Laco
Ee, Acii meya,
Kel kweyo ye,
Kella kweyo ma ogwal okiyo;

Acii liwota,
Kel kweyo wang Aringa

Anen ba;
Acii larema,
Kel kweyo,
Kel kweyo ma ogwal ongoko;

Acii meya,
Kel kweyo wek ajwaa ki laka.

Nyako
Ee, akwero kwe do maa,

Maa, wek reere, do maa?

Ee, an adeg gira,
Larac-okang lubu kor anga?

Laco
Ee, lajongo, larema,
Wacca, jal titta
Kop ma meni boko;
Kwilla, jal kwilla
Kop ma ji waco.

Nyako
Kubukubu, lubu kor anga?

Maa we! laditti kono,
Tuleke, mako bad anga?

Ai, ai, an do maa,
Lawiye otal loko kwed anga?

Give me sand

Man
Ee, Acii, my love,
Give me sand,
Give me the white sand that has been
  sieved by the frogs;

Acii, my companion,
Give me the sand from the mouth of
  the Aringa River,

Bring it, let me see it;
Acii, my friend,
Bring the white sand,
Give me the white sand that has been
  vomited by the frogs;

Acii, my love,
Give me the white sand that I may
  polish my teeth with it.

Girl
Ee, but I have rejected the man,
  mother;

Mother, but why are you so
  stubborn?

Ee, but I do not want the man,
The ugly man, the barren man,
  whom does he follow?

Man
Ee, my love, my friend,
Tell me, tell me
What your mother says;
Whisper it, whisper it to me,
Tell me what the people say.

Girl
He is bent with age,
  whom does he follow?

Mother, oh, this old man,
This rough-skinned thing,
  how can he hold my hand?
Oh, oh, me, oh, mother,
The bald-headed man,

Laco
Ee, Acii meya,
Laracci ogudu bad meya?

Ee, laditti, nye,
Cit cen, nye,
Lagedo, ngany cen,
Igin anena ku.

Nyako
Ai, ai, an do wora,
Wora, an akwero kwe do wora;

Ai, ai, an adeg gira,
Maa, an akwero acona, do maa.

Ee, laditti kono,
Oyango apika,
En ma eneko;
Okutu bila;
Ai, ai, adeg gira,
Cogo pura oneko agulu wa woko.

Laco
Ee, Acii do meya,
Kel kweyo,
Kella kweyo ma ogwal ongoko;

Acii, liwota,
Kel kweyo wang Aringa

Anen ba!

Nyako
Oraca ni kono,
Mit lim oneko wang abaa;

Man
Ee, Acii my love,
The ugly man, has he touched the
*   arm of my beloved?*
Ee, old man, listen,
Go away, do you hear?
Ugly one, limp away, you are
Too ugly to be seen.

Girl
Oh, oh, me, oh father,
Father, but I have rejected the man,
*   oh father;*
Oh, oh, I do not want the man,
Mother, I reject the old thing, oh
*   mother.*
Ee, look at the ancient thing,
He brings the guts of an animal
And claims that he was the killer,
And blows his horn;
Oh, oh, I reject him,
The bones of the antelope that he
*   brought have broken our*
*   cooking pot.*

Man
Ee, Acii, my love,
Give me sand,
Give me the white sand that has
*   been vomited by the frogs;*
Acii, my companion,
Bring me the sand from the mouth of
*   the Aringa River,*
Let me see it!

Girl
Oh, the ugly one,
The sweetness of wealth has blinded
*   my father;*

55

Laditti, nye,
Wek kong atwe yen ki maa;

Ai, ai, acona ni, nye,
Wek kong anyar raa ki maa;.

Ee, okunga ni, nye,
Kur kong aom pii ki maa.

Wora, an akwero kwe do, wora;

Won lim gire obilo abaa!

You old thing, listen,
Wait, let me first collect firewood for
my mother;
You ugly one, listen, oh,
Wait, let me first bring cooking grass
for my mother;
Oh, oh, the ugly man, oh father,
Let me fetch some water for my
mother.
Father, but I have rejected the old
man, father;
The wealthy man has bewitched my
father.

27
Lut kot go cwara

Lut kot go cwara,
Go cwara,
Wekka meya;
Ee, wekka meya;
Twolli tong cwara,
Tong cwara,
Wekka meya;
Ee, wekka meya:
    Nen ka woto,
        Nenno mitta;
    Neno ka myelo,
        Nenno mitta;
    Neno ka bunyu,
        Nenno mitta;
    Iwinyo ka kutu bila,
        Winynyo mitta;
    Iwinyo ka loko,
        Winyo mitta;
    Nen ka ucu,

        Nenno mitta;
    Nenno meya,
        Nenno mitta.
Lut kot go cwara,
Go cwara,
Wekka meya;
Ee, wekka meya.

Lightning, strike my husband

Lightning, strike my husband,
Strike my husband,
Leave my lover;
Ee, leave my lover.
Snake, bite my husband,
Bite my husband,
Leave my lover;
Ee, leave my lover.
    See him walking,
        How beautifully he walks;
    See him dancing,
        How beautifully he dances;
    See him smiling,
        How beautifully he smiles;
    Listen to the tune of his horn,
        How beautifully it sounds;
    Listen to him speaking,
        How beautifully he speaks;
    See him performing the mock-
    fight,
        How beautifully he does it;
    The sight of my lover
    Is most pleasing.
Lightning, strike my husband,
Strike my husband,
Leave my lover;
Ee, leave my lover.

Satirical Verse

'I suppose these rascals expect me to pay my own welcome . . . do they? That's fair enough. I am going to give them wine . . .' With this, he smilingly unbuttoned his handsome codpiece; and drawing out his *mentula*, he drenched them all with such bitter deluge of urine that he thereby drowned two hundred and sixty thousand four hundred and eighteen, not counting the women and children.

Rabelais: *Gargantua in Paris*

For a time the marriage was not consummated; for whenever the king went to bed with her, he was unable to have intercourse . . . This happened frequently, until at last Amasis told her that she must have bewitched him.

Herodotus: *The Histories*

28

| Maro ango? | *What mother-in-law is this?* |

Maro ango?
Ma kero calo otel
Wi yat;
Nye, Alilo,
Meni dok loko tutwal;
Uyaa, maro ango?
Ma loko calo otel

Kom got.
Alilo, kong ijuku meni
Ka lok, nye.

What mother-in-law is this?
She twitters like the woodpecker
On top of a tree;
Hey, Alilo,
Your mother talks too much.
Hey, what mother-in-law is this?
She talks endlessly like the wood-
pecker
On the hill.
Alilo, stop your mother,
Why, she talks too much.

Wan mon walony ku

Wan mon walony ku,
Walony ku ki lok pa co;

Rac araca ki wor;
Ojengo lela,
Lwonga, aye,
Cwara yeto maa,
Ayela pa co,
Rac araca ki wor;
Okako kongo oyeng,
Ngok i koma;
Walony awene?
Alany pa co,
Rac araca ki wor;
Ot bene ononga alilo ma ber,
Cwara neno ku,
Lok pa co,
Rac araca ki wor:
Otingo twon nyac ki i boma,

Bino rado i koma,
Wan walony ku,
Arem pa two,
Rac araca ki wor;
Nyodo bene yang anongo,
Cwara leyo wiya,
Ki lok ming ming,
Rac araca ki wor;
Wan mon walony ku,
Walony ku ki lok pa co,

Rac araca ki wor.

We women will never have peace

We women will never have peace,
We will never prosper, the troubles
from men are ceaseless,
At night they are worse.
He stands his bicycle,
He calls me, I respond,
My man hurls insults at my mother;
The troubles from men are ceaseless,
At night they are worse.
He drinks to his full,
And vomits on me;
When shall we have peace?
The troubles from men are ceaseless,
At night they are worse;
My house is spotlessly clean,
My man does not see it,
The troubles from men are ceaseless,
At night they are worse;
He carries a bull gonorrhoea from the
town
And smears it in my body,
We shall never have peace,
The pain is terrible,
At night it is worse.
I even bore him children,
My man bothers my head
With stupid words,
At night he is worse;
We women will never have peace,
We will never prosper, the troubles
from men are ceaseless,
At night they are worse.

30

Abedo mera ataa

Abedo mera ataa
Ka gwoko gang,
Atwom oneka ye,
Onangnang nango labutubutu;

Malaya otima nye,
Atworo toka ataa
Ka lilo ot,
Onangnang otima ba,
Onangnang nango labutubutu.
Atwom oneka,
An aturu kora
Ka twomo pii,
Lok man cwero cwinya,
Lubeco mogo nango labutubutu,

Malaya obwoli nye,

Atalo cinga ata
Ka rego moko,
Onangnang obiti ye,
Lukwele wai nango labutubutu;

Atwom oneka nyong,

Awango cinga ata
Ka tedo nguny,
Malaya omati ye,

Onangnang mato labutubutu,

Cwara, atoo mera ata
Ka pito pit,
Malaya otyeki ye,

Onangnang nango labutubutu.

Here I am

Here I am
Looking after my home,
The burden is killing me, oh;
And the suckers are sucking, lying on
their beds.

The prostitutes treat me badly;
Here I am,
Making my house spotlessly clean,
The suckers treat me badly,
They are sucking, lying on their beds.
The burden is killing me,
I break my back
Carrying water from the well,
I am so sad;
The beautiful ones are sucking, lying
on their beds.

The prostitutes deceive you, but
listen,
The skin of my hands is hardened
Grinding the millet,
And the suckers tell you lies, oh,
The loose women are sucking, lying
on their beds.

The burden is killing me, I get
nothing for it;
My hands are burnt
Cooking for you,
And the prostitutes are drinking all
your money.

The suckers are sucking, lying on
their beds;

Husband, I kill myself
Feeding our children,
And the prostitutes are finishing you,
oh,
The suckers are sucking, lying on
their beds.

Tik-tik-tik ki labenu

At least, I came with a goatskin skirt

Tik-tik-tik ki labenu,

Gangngi onywara nye;
Gang pa co nywaro dano ye,

In ceng ibwola ki ngo?
Gang pa co yelo dano,
Gangngi oyela nye;
Onongo ceng abino ki labelete,

Gangngi oronyo an;
Gang pa co ronyo dano do;

Ot pa co baro wiya,
Gang pa co balo wiya,
Gang man oyela nye.
Onongo ceng abino ki latin do,
Joni oyeta ye;
Gang pa co cayo dano do;
In ceng ibila ki ngo?
Gang pa co yelo dano,
Gang man oyela ye.

At least, I came with a goatskin skirt;
This home has insulted me;
The homes of men heap insults on women;
With what did you deceive me?
The homes of men trouble women,
This home has troubled me much.
At least I came with a small loin cloth, oh,
This home has ashamed me;
The homes of men fill women with shame;
This house gives me headache,
This home troubles my head,
The home has troubled me much, oh.
When I came, I had a child;
These people have abused me, oh,
The homes of men laugh at women;
With what did you bewitch me?
The homes of men trouble women,
This home has troubled me much, oh.

32

An tin abutu kena

An tin abutu kena;
Cwara tin orii
Ka mato kongo,
Dwogo ku;
Maa, an tin abutu kena;
Laco okako kongo omer
Dong bonga ku;
Lutua, an tin abutu kena;
Laco omato kongo oyeny,
Dong lokka ngeye;
Jone, an tin abutu kena,
Cwara tin omato kongo omer
Tin butu ni lede.

Last night I slept alone

Last night I slept alone,
My man was away,
    drinking,
He would not come home;
Mother, last night I slept alone,
My man was totally drunk,
He would not touch me;
My clansmen, last night I slept alone,
My man was drunk,
He turned his back to me;
My people, last night I slept alone,
My man was drunk,
He slept like a corpse.

33

Omato kongo oyeng	*The man is drunk*

Omato kongo oyeng,
Dong yenyo mon;
Jalli omato kongo omer
Me layel mon;

The man is drunk,
And is looking for women;
He is drunk
And wants to trouble women for
nothing;

Laco okako kongo oyeng
Dong bwolo mon,

The man is totally drunk,
He is deceiving women, he can't do
it;

Jal atongo cuni ki lukile,
Atono dudumaki iye;
Laco omato kongo omer
Yela nono;
Lebelebelebe lubu kor anga?

Man, I will cut off your penis,
And put insecticide in the wound.
The man is drunk,
He is troubling me for nothing;
His penis is flabby and shrunken,
who is he following?

Jal atongo dudi ki lukile,

Man, I will split your back with an
axe

Abalo ot nyodoni woko.
Omato kongo oyeng
Me layel mon.

And destroy the store of your sperm;
The man is totally drunk,
He wants to bother women for
nothing.

34

Lawino kuru keya	*Lawino is waiting for a soldier*
Lawino kuru keya,	*Lawino is waiting for a soldier;*
Olang kok ni tili;	*The bells are pealing;*
Lamingi kara kuru keya;	*The foolish one is waiting for a soldier;*
Olang okok;	*Bells are ringing;*
Lawino kara kwiya keya,	*Lawino must be ignorant about soldiers,*
Ee, lapangcata kuru keya.	*Ee, the stupid one is waiting for a soldier.*

35

Mon keya lulur

Mon keya lulur,
Kerekerekere ki waraga,
Waraga doko latin ce?
Mon keya lulur.

Soldiers' wives are barren

Soldiers' wives are barren;
They are always writing letters,
Can letters become children?
Soldiers' wives are barren.

36

Ceng apako ni dereva	*I thought he was a driver*
Ceng apako ni dereva,	*I thought he was a driver,*
Kara pe ye;	*But he is not;*
Ato woko;	*I wish I were dead;*
Lanyanni oye panyako ye;	*This woman has fallen in love*
	with a mere carrier, oh,
Ceng apako ni dereva.	*I thought he was a driver.*

37
Twon nyac ma lakeya

Twon nyac ma lakeya
Orado kom lakeya;

Lakeya kok, oyoyo,
Kok benebene;
Twon cun lakeya,

Obako ki lakeya,
Anyaka kok oyoyo,
Kok benebene.

The bull gonorrhoea

The bull gonorrhoea
That the soldier smeared in the body
of my aunt's daughter;
My aunt's daughter cries oh, oh, oh,
She cries all night long.
The huge penis with which the
soldier
Speared my aunt's daughter,
My aunt's daughter cries oh, oh, oh,
She cries all night long.

Nen min Opoka

Nen min Opoka,
Oloko doge kunyango,
Oloko ngeye kupoto ceng
Ka kok do;
Omako wiy ki cinge aryo;
Lanyongonyongo ye,
Wer tum ku,
Omako wiye ting-ting,
Onyongo cuny ka kok do.

Look at Opoka's mother

Look at Opoka's mother,
Her mouth is turned to the east,
Her back towards sunset,
She is weeping, oh,
Holding her head with both hands,
And squatting,
She is singing endlessly,
And holding her head tightly,
She is squatting and crying.

39

Anongo nyer mo	*I found a certain man*
Anongo nyer mo	*I found a certain man*
Tye ka pwonyo nyare,	*Advising his daughter*
Gwok oyee la-can;	*Not to marry a poor man;*
Anongo jal moni	*I found a certain man*
Tye ka pwonyo nyare,	*Telling his daughter*
Gwok oyee la-can;	*Not to marry a poor man;*
La-can bene dano,	*But a poor man is a human being*
Lalonyo bene dano,	*And a rich man is also a human being;*
Danni ducuducu dano pa Lubanga.	*All human beings are God's people.*

Ajuc man ka oneno awobe

Ajuc man ka oneno awobe,

Tude, tude calo twon latal,

Tude do;
Ajucci ka owinyo pi co,

Tude, tude, bolo latek i ococ,

Tude do.

*This old woman when she sees
   young men*

*This old woman, when she sees young
   men,*

*She jumps, she jumps like a bull
   wizard,*

She jumps, oh ;

*This old woman, when she hears
   about men,*

*She jumps, she jumps, and throws her
   smoking pipe in the hole
   in the anthill,*

She jumps.

41

Uyeny yat mutwo	*Get a dry peg*
Uyeny yat mutwo,	*Get a dry peg,*
Urwak i ter Owiny;	*Drive it through Owiny's anus;*
Twon lajokki,	*The bull wizard is*
Twora Lunyama;	*Fiercer than Lunyama;*
Uyeny yat ma bor,	*Get a long peg,*
Urwak i ter Owiny,	*Drive it through Owiny's anus;*
Twora Lunyama,	*Much fiercer then Lunyama,*
Lajokki oneko piny.	*He has killed the land.*

42

Upeny Barakia	*You people, ask Barakia*
Upeny Barakia,	*You people, ask Barakia,*
Nongo dako kwene?	*Where will he get a wife?*
Dica we,	*You Dica,*
Twon lajokki	*This bull witch,*
Nongo dako kwene?	*Where will he get a wife?*
Lawiye odin,	*The bushy-headed man,*
Ee, okwongo ki i minne.	*Ee, he was already a witch*
	in his mother's womb.

43

Ululula, maa, woda do

Ululula, maa, woda do!

Twon jok pa joni,
Neko oda;
Jok Paibona,
Jok oyengo agulu li-kijikijikiji!

Mother, listen

*Mother, listen to my ululation; my
son, oh!
The witchcraft of these people
Has killed my household;
The witchcraft of Paibona people
Shakes the pot like an earthquake.*

44
Dyang doge lac

Dyang doge lac,
Dyang okelo lawol i gang;

Awobe maku odo.
Dyang okelo ma calo kwac;

Orobo tua,
Gwok unek dako.
Dyang okelo lawol i paco,

Dyang doge lac.

Cattle have wide mouths

Cattle have wide mouths,
*Cattle have brought a poison woman
    into the homestead;*
Young men, take your whips.
*Cattle have brought a woman
    beautiful and dangerous as a
    leopard;*
Youths of our clan,
Do not kill the woman.
*Cattle have brought a poison woman
    into our homestead,*
Cattle have wide mouths.

45

Wange otoo wa con

Wange otoo wa con,
Polo nen ki iye;
Too wang lapwony,
Polo nen do;
Wange otoo con;
Lapwony weko maraya ku;

Wange otoo con,
Polo nen ki iye.

His eyes died long ago

His eyes died long ago,
You can see clouds in them;
The death of the eyes of the teacher,
Clouds are visible in them, oh;
His eyes died long ago;
*The teacher does not leave his glasses
    behind;*

His eyes died long ago,
You can see clouds in them.

46

In ibedo ki nyero li-kak kak-kak

In ibedo ki nyero li-kak-kak-kak,
Dako kono peke;
Ee, omera ma yengo gica;

Omera ma myelo myel arima,
Nono, dako pare peke;
Jalli okelo dako ma
Kwac omato iye,

Nywal ku kwak;
Jalli okelo dako ma iye ojing con

Calo dul kijing;
Omera ma kelo dul okeco;
Ee, omera ma myelo myel arima,

Omera ni yengo gica nono,

Dako pare peke,
Jalli okelo dako
Ma kwac omato iye

Nywal ku kwak.

You keep on laughing and laughing

You keep on laughing and laughing,
Yet you have no wife;
Ee, this brother who shakes his
headgear,
My brother who dances so vigorously,
Is a nobody, he has no wife;
He has brought home a woman
Whose womb has been sucked by a
leopard,
She cannot bear a child;
This man has brought home a woman
whose womb was hardened long ago,
Hard like a piece of kijing wood,
Like a piece of okeco wood;
Ee, this brother who dances so
vigorously,
My brother who shakes his headgear,
is a nobody,
He has no wife;
This man has brought home a woman
Whose womb has been sucked by a
leopard,
She can never have a child.

47
Rii rii ye

Rii rii ye,
Rii rii ye,
Awinyo lela okok,
Lela okok kili,
Meno nya pa nga?
Lim kor Laker,
Lim kor lamera,
Iwilo ki gari ba:
Awinyo lela okok,
Lela okok kili,
Kelo dako bongo?

Rii rii ye,
Lim kor Laker,
Inyomo ki gari ba?
Awinyo lela okok,
Wang lela peke,
Konyo dano bongo;
Lajwaa oboli,

Lim kor lamera,
Inyomo ki gari ba,
Iomo lela mwa,

Tun lela lal,
Rombo cundi bongo.

I hear a bicycle bell

I hear a bicycle bell,
I hear a bicycle bell,
The bell sounded,
It went kling-kling,
Whose daughter is that?
The bridewealth of Laker,
The bridewealth of my sister,
You use for buying a bicycle;
I hear a bicycle bell,
It went kling-kling,
*Why does it not bring a woman
    home?*

I hear a bicycle bell,
The bridewealth of Laker,
Why do you marry a bicycle with it?
I hear a bicycle bell,
A bicycle has no eyes,
It cannot help your clansmen;
*You man who was knocked down by
    an antelope,*
The bridewealth of my sister,
You use it for marrying a bicycle,
*You have brought a bicycle home for
    nothing;*
The bicycle's vagina
Is too small for your penis.

Songs of the Spirit Possession Dance

Ancient the wood stands
Unhewn for many a season
It seems some presence dwells
Within the grove.

Ovid: *Metamorphoses*

When the unclean spirit has gone out of a man,
he passes through waterless places seeking rest;
and finding none he says, 'I will return to my
house from which I came'.

St Luke XI 24

48

Ogengo nyara nywal	*It made my daughter barren*
Ogengo nyara nywal ye,	*It made my daughter barren, oh,*
Kop pa Kulu,	*Spirit of the Stream is responsible,*
Ya we, ya we;	*Oh yes, oh yes;*
Nyodo ber ki obeno,	*Childbirth is good; let me strap the baby on my back,*
Kop pa Kulu,	*Spirit of the Stream is responsible,*
Ya we, ya we;	*Oh yes, oh yes;*
Kulu, gwok iloona iya;	*Spirit of the Stream, do not destroy my pregnancy;*
Maa, Kulu,	*Mother, Spirit of the Stream,*
Ya we, ya we.	*Oh yes, oh yes.*

49

Twon gweno pa Kulu en	*Here is a cock for the Spirit of the Stream*
Twon gweno pa Kulu en,	*Here is a cock for the Spirit of the Stream,*
Eiya, eiya;	*Oh yes, oh yes;*
Kic bene mit me ananga,	*Honey is also required, for eating,*
Eiya, eiya;	*Oh yes, oh yes;*
Labolo mitte me amwonya,	*And bananas, for swallowing,*
Eiya, eiya;	*Oh yes, oh yes;*
An akayo wiye,	*I bite a piece of it,*
Eiya, eiya.	*Oh yes, oh yes.*

50

Owiny lee tim

Owiny lee tim
Ma woto ma dano;
Owiny omera
Jok lum,
Owiny lee tim
Ma woto ma dano.

Owiny is a wild beast

Owiny is a wild beast
That goes about like a man;
Owiny is my brother,
He is a spirit of the bush;
Owiny is a wild beast
That goes about like a man.

51

Anongo dyang kwene?	*Where shall I find a bull?*
Anongo dyang kwene	*Where shall I find a bull*
Amii ki omera?	*To present to my brother?*
Omera, an awoto ki latwol,	*My brother, I have come with a white cock,*
Ki lamola;	*And some lamola simsim;*
An awoto ki latwol;	*I have come with a white cock;*
Cwara woto yon,	*My husband is away, strutting on the pathways,*
An anongo dyang kwene	*Where shall I find a bull*
Amii ki omera?	*To present to my brother?*

52

Omera yam won ngom

Omera yam won ngom,
Otwala ye,
Nen ka abako doga;
Omera ye,
Won bangi ye,
Won ngom,
Nen abedo wi kom ker;

Won Ocen gikwed Opiyo,
Omera ma yam won ngom,
Winy ka abako doga.

My brother who ruled the land

My brother who ruled the land,
Otwala, oh,
Look at me praying to you;
My brother, oh,
Father of twins, oh,
Ruler of the land,
*Look at me sitting on the chiefly
    stool;*
Father of Ocen and Opiyo,
My brother who ruled the land,
Listen to me praying to you.

53

Lapul ki kolo pare	*Lapul in its anger*
Lapul ki kolo pare,	*Lapul in its anger*
Mako we ki okeyo;	*Possesses even maternal uncles;*
Jok man wai lakolo;	*This Spirit is an angry one,*
Mako wa ki nero,	*It possesses even paternal uncles;*
Lapul ki kolo pare,	*Lapul in its impertinence*
Mako wa ki omaro.	*Possesses even the children of sisters.*

54

Awero Omarari	*I sing to Omarari*
Awero Omarari do,	*I sing to Omarari, oh,*
Awero Omarari do, oo;	*I sing to Omarari, oh, oh;*
Omarari wek kolo obedi,	*Omarari, let your anger abate;*
Awero Omarari do;	*I sing to Omarari, oh,*
Kitino ma tye,	*Omarari, let your wrath cease;*
Kitino pa Omarari;	*The children that are here*
Awobe ma tye,	*Are Omarari's children;*
Awobe pa Omarari;	*The boys that are here*
	are Omarari's boys;
Nyako ma tye,	*Any girl here*
Nyako pa Omarari;	*Belongs to Omarari;*
Awero Omarari,	*I sing to Omarari,*
Omarari wek kolo obedi.	*Omarari, let your anger abate.*

55

Jok ker wai mito nyako	*The chiefly spirit desires a girl*
Jok ker wai mito nyako;	*The chiefly spirit desires a girl;*
Jok kwaro,	*Spirit of old,*
Jok wa, ka imito nyako,	*You spirit that belongs to us,*
	if you desire a girl,
Amii mola en;	*Here, I present you with a brass bangle;*
Lapul, ka imito nyako,	*Lapul, you desire a girl,*
Amii mola en.	*Here, I present you with a brass bangle.*

56

Aligo ye

Aligo ye,
Cwara dwogo awene?
Aligo ye,
Cwar mon alwak;
Cwara ma woto wor,
Cwara dwogo awene?
Cwar mon kibwoya.

Lone hunter, oh

Lone hunter, oh,
When will my husband return home?
Lone hunter, oh,
Husband of many wives,
My husband goes about at night;
When will my husband return home?
Husband of defeated wives.

57

Otwala, cwar mon alwak	*Otwala, husband of many wives*
Otwala, cwar mon alwak,	*Otwala, husband of many wives,*
Otwala, kolo pare ido do;	*Otwala, his anger is being provoked;*
Otwala, kwac pa Nyaga ye,	*Otwala, leopard of Nyago, oh,*
Otwala, kolo pare bino do:	*Otwala, his anger is coming, oh;*
Otwala, cwar mon ma beco	*Otwala, husband of beautiful wives,*
Otwala, kolo pare ido do.	*Otwala, his anger is coming, oh.*

58

Twon co woto aligo

Twon co woto aligo,

Meno cwara ku;
Ladwar woto aligo ye;

Anong cwara mo kwene?
Twon co ma woto aligo,

Meno cwara ku.

*The bull of men that goes
hunting alone*

*The bull of men that goes hunting
alone,*
That is not my husband;
*The hunter that goes hunting alone,
oh;*
Where can I find a man?
*The bull of men that goes hunting
alone,*
That is not my husband.

59

Tong ma lake tek	*The spear with the hard point*

Tong ma lake tek,
Kako lela;
Tong ma yam ageno,
Baro lela;
Ladwar obutu i tim,
Ato woko;
Tong ma yam ageno,
Kako lela;
Tong ma lake bit,
Cubu lela;
Aligo tongnge tek,
Ato woko;
Ladwar obutu i tim,
Ato woko;
Tong ma yam ageno,
Baro got.

The spear with the hard point,
Let it split the granite rock;
The spear that I trust,
Let it split the granite rock;
The hunter has slept in the wilderness,
I am dying, oh;
The spear that I trust,
Let it split the granite rock;
The spear with the sharp point,
Let it crack the granite rock;
The hunter's spear is sharp,
I am dying, oh;
The hunter has slept in the wilderness,
I am dying, oh;
The spear that I trust,
Let it split the granite rock.

Chants at the Ancestral Shrine

Go, kill a black chicken.
Prepare it and offer it.
Go forth, and offer it on the main roads . . .
Let not evil's combings fall on us.
Let them fall amidst the trees of the woods
Or elsewhere: the country is spacious . . .

Thai funeral poem

Against your children, father elephant
Do not be angry . . .
My lance of sharpened iron, honour to you.

Pygmy hunting song

60

| Kwaro tin dong oloko | *The ancestors have spoken today* |

<table>
<tr><td>

Won abila
Kwaro tin dong oloko;
Uyeny nyok kibworo,
Gweno ki kongo.

</td><td>

Elder
The ancestors have spoken today;
Bring forth a brown billy goat,
Chicken and beer.

</td></tr>
<tr><td>

Wora, ceng ikoko cam,
Cammi tin en;
Bin iye dong;
Lwong omegini ducu;
Camwu en.

</td><td>

My father, you have asked for food;
Your food is here today;
Come to it now;
Call all your brothers,
Your food is here.

</td></tr>
<tr><td>

Wun lukaka,
An alwongo wun
Pi wego ma atedo;

</td><td>

You my clansmen and clanswomen,
I have called you
Because of the food I have cooked for
   our fathers;

</td></tr>
<tr><td>

Biyu, wamiyu igi cam.
Tin amako dyel en,
Wamiyu ki wora.

</td><td>

Come, let us give them food.
Today I hold a goat in my hand,
Let us give it to my father.

</td></tr>
<tr><td>

Kwaro,
Wuyee cam ma wamiyo iwu tin;
Camwu dong en.
Walworowu pingo?
Wun luditowa,
Nyokwu tin en;
Tin dong wumat remo.
Gemo ma bino owok ki tenge.

</td><td>

You, our fathers,
Accept the food we give you today;
Here is your food.
Why should we fear you?
You are our fathers.
Your billy goat is here,
Drink its blood today.
The fiends that are coming
   let them pass far away.

</td></tr>
<tr><td>

Camwu en.
Kitino komgi kubed yot;
Mon gunong nyodo,
Wek nyingwu pe kurweny;

</td><td>

Your food is here today.
Let your children have good health;
Let the women have good childbirth,
So that your name may not be
   obliterated.

</td></tr>
<tr><td>

Gwenowu en;
Remo dong tin wamiyo iwu en.
Komwa kubed ma yot.
Too obed peke i paco.

</td><td>

Your chicken is here;
Today we give you blood.
Let us have good health;
Let there be no deaths in the
   homestead.

</td></tr>
<tr><td>

Kano yang wan wapeke,

</td><td>

If we were not here,

</td></tr>
</table>

Kono cam bene peke.	*There would be no food for you.*
Kongo wamiyo dong en;	*Here, we give you beer;*
Kom dano obed ma yot,	*Let us have good health,*
Two ma bino kuwok ki tenge.	*Diseases that are coming,*
	let them pass far away.

Tin amii dyel,	*Today, I give you a goat;*
Tin amii remo;	*Today, I give you blood;*
Tin amii kongo,	*Today, I give you beer;*
Amii kongo me kweyo orwooni.	*I give you beer to quench your thirst.*

Komwa obed ma yot.	*Let us have good health.*
Wuling eno ba;	*Let there be silence, oh;*
Wuling mot.	*Let there be silence.*
Wan tin watedo wora;	*Today, we have cooked a feast for my father;*

Tin amiye cam;	*Today, I have given him food;*
Ento wuling mot.	*But, let there be silence.*
Kom dano kubed ma yot.	*Let the people have good health.*

Lwak	All
Kom dano kubed ma yot.	*Let the people have good health.*

Won abila	Elder
Ngu otoo.	*Let the lions be killed.*

Lwak	All
Otoo, otoo, otoo.	*Let them be killed, killed, killed.*

Won abila	Elder
Tong obed ma bit.	*Let our spears be sharp and straight.*

Lwak	All
Ma bit, bit, bit.	*Let them be sharp, sharp, and straight.*

Won abila	Elder
Nyodo opot kom kitino mon.	*Let the women have good childbirth.*

Lwak	All
Opoti, opoti, opoti.	*Let them have good childbirth.*

Won abila	Elder
Cam otwii ma ber, cam oceki.	*Let the crops germinate well,*
	let the crops ripen well.

Won abila
Cam otwii ma ber, cam oceki.

Elder
Let the crops germinate well,
let the crops ripen well.

Lwak
Oceki, oceki, oceki.

All
Let the crops germinate and ripen
well.

Won abila
Litino okoki, ngwee, ngwee, ngwee.

Elder
Let the children's cries be heard.

Lwak
Ngwee, ngwee, ngwee.

All
Let them be heard, heard, heard.

Won abila
Gigu ma racu ma i paco,

Wang ceng oter.

Elder
The evil things that are in the
homestead,
Let the setting sun take them down
in the west.

Lwak
Wang ceng oter.

All
Let it take, take, take.

Won abila
Wang ceng oter.

Elder
Let the setting sun take them.

Lwak
Oter.

All
Let it take.

Won abila
Oter.

Elder
Let it take.

Lwak
Oter.

All
Let it take.

Won abila
Wang ceng oter.

Elder
Let the setting sun take them.

Lwak
Ci otero.

All
And so it has taken them.

61

Lutua, an alwongowu ka kwero lyec

Won abila

Lutua, an alwongowu ka kwero
  lyec en;
Ka lyec obino, ci obin mukwee.

Lwak
Obino, ci obin mukwee.

Won abila
In lakwor mewa, merok,

Ito lakucel.

Lwak
Obino, ci obin mukwee.

Won abila
Kit ma man dok oketo wiye ka ma
  con,
Mukene dok obin.

Lwak
Obin, ci obin mukwee.

Won abila
In merok, lakwor ma con.

Itoo lakucel.
Too mot;
Bin mukwe.

Lwak
Bin, ci ibin mukwe.

Won abila
An alamo doga bot kwaro;
Latin tin okelo wi lyec paco

Kit ma wun ludito ceng utimo.

*My clansmen, I have called you
  to pacify this elephant*

Elder
*My clansmen, I have called you to
  pacify this elephant.
As the elephant has come,
  let it come in peace.*

All
It has come, but let it come in peace.

Elder
*There is a feud between you and us;
  you are our enemy;
Your death will not be avenged.*

All
It has come, but let it come in peace.

Elder
*As this has laid its head where others
  laid theirs,
Let more others come.*

All
Let them come, but come in peace.

Elder
*You are our enemy; there is a feud
  between us;*

*You will die unavenged.
Die peacefully;
Come in peace.*

All
Come, but come in peace.

Elder
*I pray to the ancestors:
This child has brought the head of an
  elephant home
As you used to do.*

Latin kome obed ma yot.
Gigu ma racu ma mito bino,
Poto ceng oter woko.

Yat ma i tim ma latin ocoore
    ikome,
Yat onacce woko, owek yoo obed
    ma leng.

Uyaa, wan tin watimo gin paco,

Nyodo obin yo;
Litino ci okoki, ngwee, ngwee,
    ngwee.
Wun Ludongo, nenu,
Latin tin okelo wi lyec.

En En

Lyec, in jok ma i tim;

Tin lukeli paco;

Tin dong lukweyi ki romo en.

Dong ibed ma ber;
Lwong luwediwu, gubin, gutoo
    calo in.
Wii okel luwoti.
Amii wee,
Amii kongo,
Amii nyim ki peke;
Lwong luwediwu ducu.

Let the child have good health;
Evil things that are coming,
Let the setting sun take them down in
    the west;
A tree in the bush against which this
    child might knock and hurt himself.
Let the tree bend away and leave his
    path clear.

Listen, as today we have purified this
    homestead,
Let childbirth come, oh;
Let the cries of children be heard;

You elders, see to it.
This child has brought the head of an
    elephant today;
Here it is.

You elephant,
    you are a spirit of the bush;
Today we have brought you into the
    homestead;
Today, you have been pacified with this
    ram.
Now, come with a good heart.
Call all your companions,
    let them come, and die like you;
Let your head invite your companions.
I give you chyme;
I give you beer;
I give you simsim and peas:
Call all your companions.

Songs of War

A great and wrathful contest is shaping.

Sophocles: *Ajax*

I shall pounce on them like a falcon;
I kill them, I slaughter them, I crush them to the earth.

Egyptian: *The battle of Kadesh*

Rise the spear and draw the sword.
Smite the neck and pierce the side.
The blood is gushing purple

Burma: *Song of a war band*

Tero dano i gul Acaa

Ee, tero dano i gul Acaa,

Morongole, lwak pa Piromoi
Tero dano i gul nam;
Oh, yooo, oh, Lumorogelo,
Tongwa romo Lumorogelo;
Ee, tero dano i romo mony,

Morongole, lwak pa Piromoi
Cubu dano i gul Acaa,

Oh, oyooo, oh, Lumorogelo,
Tongwa romo Lumorogelo

He leads his men towards the bend of the Acaa River

He leads his men towards the bend of the Acaa River,
Morongole, the host of Piromoi,
Moves towards the bend of the River
Oh, yes, at Lumorogelo,
Our spears will clash at Lumorogelo;
Ee, he leads his men towards the final assault,
Morongole, the host of Piromoi
Will slaughter men at the bend of the Acaa River;
Oh, yes, at Lumorogelo,
Our spears will clash at Lumorogelo.

63

Kakare rac	*The place was awful*

Kakare rac,
Co olal i koo;
Kakare rac,
Co olal i koo;
Co otum i koo, do nye,

Co otum bot Piribong,
Piribong odong i apulu;
Ribiribi, Lumoi,
Agola Lumoi,

Kakare rac.

The place was awful,
Men perished in the bamboo forest;
The place was awful,
Men perished in the bamboo forest;
Men were slaughtered in the bamboo
    forest,

The warriors of Piribong were finished,
And Piribong was left in the dust;
Lumoi, listen to the drumming footsteps
Of the escaping warrirors; Agola
    Lumoi,

The place was awful.

64

| Palaro gin acel, aryo | *The host of Palaro, only a few,* |

Palaro gin acel, aryo . . .

Otingo polo ki tere;
Ee, Lango ringo,
Otingo polo ki tere;
Palaro gin acel, aryo . . .

Oyengo kidi wi Lango;
Ee, Lango kok ca,
Otingo polo ki tere.

The host of Palaro, only a few,
 you can count them
The host of Palaro,
 only a few, you can count them,
Lifted the sky from its base;
Ee, the Lango fled;
They lifted the sky from its base.
The host of Palaro,
 only a few, you can count them,
Shook the mountain on the Lango,
Ee, the Lango wailed;
They lifted the sky from its base.

65

Tong romo ki wedi	*Spears clashed with spears*
Tong romo ki wedi ye,	*Spears clashed with spears, oh;*
Ilamo lapii kwe;	*In vain you invoked your luck.*
Oboke olwedo,	*The leaves of the olwedo tree,*
Oboke olwedo mukoni;	*It was the leaves of the olwedo tree that saved you.*
Lweny ma Ogwal Lameny ywaa ye,	*In the battle led by Ogwal Lameny, oh,*
Oweko Omiro owang imac	*Omiro were burnt in the fire*
Ame pura;	*Like kongonis;*
Oyoo, Omiro, oweko Omiro owang i mac	*Oh, Omiro, Omiro were burnt in the fire*
Ame pura.	*Like kongonis.*

66
La-lworo dok i meni

La-lworo dok i meni,

Kodi pa luming,
Kodi pa lugingi,
La-lworo ogengo ira yoo ding;

Nga ma lwongo nyinga
Omo lok ming?
Kodi pa luming,

La-lworo ogengo ira yoo ding;

La-lworo dok i meni.

Coward, crawl back into your mother's womb

Coward, crawl back into your mother's womb
We are sons of the brave,
Sons of stubborn people.
The coward has blocked my path completely.
Who is that calling my name
And arguing stupidly?
We are sons of the brave, sons of stubborn people,
The coward has blocked my path completely;
Coward, crawl back into your mother's womb.

Tongwa cobo nguny jo

Ee, kura abin anen tongwa do,
Ee, ocubu nguny jo
Ma ronyo wa,
Tongwa ye,
Ee, tongwa do,
Ee, cubu nguny jo
Ma ronyo wa.

Our spears pierce the anus

Ee, wait, let me find our spears,
Ee, they pierce the anus of the people
Who insult us;
Our spears, oh,
Ee, our spears,
Ee, they pierce the anus of the people
Who insult us.

68

Aliker, kel dyanga

Aliker, kel dyanga,
Ka ilwor,
Mony Gala, cung ikura,

Waiwaromo Lamola.
Iyoo, Mulaji lwor, dako loyo;

Mulaji lwor, ee, Agwe dako loyo;

Mulaji lwor, Mulaji lwor, pyelo i
  kaki;
Aliker, kel dyanga.

Aliker, return my cattle

Aliker, return my cattle;
But if you are a coward,
Tell your white allies to halt, and wait
  for me,
We shall meet at Lamola.
Oh yes, Mulaji is a coward, a woman
  defeats him;
Mulaji is a coward, a coward, he
  exretes in his trousers.
Mulaji is a coward, ee, Agwe is
  defeated by a woman.
Aliker, return my cattle.

69

Lakila kelo mony me lanek Oyuru

Lakila kelo mony me lanek Oyuru,
Tum pa Kakila okok te Lacic;

Ee, Lakila ero mony aka, eiyee;

Nok rac ocera lweny,

Oneko Oyuru ye,
Nok rac ocera lweny do, eiyee;

Lakila ywayo mony me lanek Oyuru.

Lakila started a fight to kill Oyuru

Lakila started a fight to kill Oyuru,
His trumpet sounded at the foot of Lacic Hill;

Ee, Lakila started the fight deliberately, eh;

It is bad to be few, that is why I did not fight;

He killed Oyuru, oh,
It is bad to be few, that is why I did not fight;

Lakila led his hosts into battle to kill Oyuru.

70
Obako kono

Obako kono ye,

Wod Lango obako kono;

Labongo oneko awobi
  ma pune kigoro ye,
Oo, kigoro,
Labongo oneko awobi ma lapyem.

Obako kono ye.

*He had donned a huge
  headdress*
*He had donned a huge ostrich-feather
  headdress;*
*The young warrior from Lango
  had a huge headdress.*
*Labongo killed the warrior with killer
  marks on his legs, oh,*
With killer marks on his legs.
*Labongo killed the young warrior
  who used to boast;*
*He had donned a huge ostrich-feather
  headdress.*

Mony ocoro kulu kweyo

Mony ocoro kulu kweyo,
Wayelle;
Mony yang coro kunyango?

Mony pa Agwe gikwed Eliya
Muneko Urule;
Lagony oito wi kana;
In Agwe yang ipyem,
Mony ocoro kulu kweyo,
Wayelle;
Mony yang coro kunyango?

The enemy has crossed the sandy river

The enemy has crossed the sandy river,
Rise, let us do something;
What enemy ever attacked from the east?

The host of Agwe and Eliya
That killed Urule;
Lagony is mounted on an ass.
You, Agwe, you used to boast;
The enemy has skirted the sandy river,
Rise, let us do something.
What enemy ever attacks from the east?

Tongnga romo iya	*I trust my spear*
Tongnga romo iya,	*I trust my spear,*
Maya lwor;	*The Maya are cowards;*
Orobo tua camo nyikwara	*Our men will earn battle honours*
Kom got;	*In the battle on the hill;*
Ee, i Akara, ee,	*Ee, on Akara hill, ee,*
Ayelu luneko, ee, i Akara,	*Ayelu is dead, ee, on Akara,*
Ayelu yee,	*Ayelu, oh,*
Tonga romo iya,	*I trust my spear,*
Maya lwor.	*The Maya are cowards.*

73

Parajok obino rom mani?

Parajok obino rom mani?

Koro pe;
Lwak pare, Lubai coko lwak pare
Bino to;
Ee, ayaa,
Parajok obino rom mani?

Pany cunya ye,
Alaro ayaa,
Gala obino;
Parajok obino rom mani?

The army of Parajok is advancing, how large is it?

The army of Parajok is advancing, how large is it?
The people of Koro are no more.
His host, Lubai is gathering his host,
He is advancing undeterred;
Ee, mother,
The army of Parajok is advancing, how large is it?
I feel pain in my breast bone,
I run to my mother;
The Gala are advancing,
The army of Parajok is advancing, how large is it?

74

Payira mito lworo

Payira seems overwhelmed by fear

Payira mito lworo,
Abok oywayo mony tero kom Palaro;
Payira wek lworo;
Palaro otoro komgi,
Payira mito lworo.

Payira seems overwhelmed by fear,
Abok leads his host against Palaro;
Payira, stop your cowardice;
Palaro have closed their ranks,
And Payira seems overwhelmed by fear.

75
Okelo kome

Okelo kome,
Adyerri ye,
Ee, lwak pa Wangale,
Okelo kome te Akwang ye;

Tiria balo ki arima;

Ee, lwak pa Wangale,
Ee, kitino pa Onyang, nye,
Gwok wubal ki arima;
Okelo kome te Akwang ye.

The enemy has exposed his body

The enemy has exposed his body,
I will leave him for you,
Ee, host of Wangale,
*The enemy has exposed his body at the
    foot of Akwang hill, oh;*
*Young warriors, do not spoil things by
    impatience.*
Ee, host of Wangale,
Children of Onyang, listen,
Do not spoil things by impatience,
*The enemy has exposed his body at the
    foot of Akwang hill.*

76

| Lweny ma Lengamoi ywa | *In the battle led by Lengamoi* |

Lweny ma Lengamoi ywaa ye,
Opoo Awai oyango rwot
Ame lee tim;
Oboke olwedo,
Oboke olwedo muume;

Tong romo ki wedi ye!
Ilamo lapii kwe.
Lweny ma Lengamoi ywaa ye,
Jo Patongo owang i mac

Ame lee tim.

In the battle led by Lengamoi, oh,
Opoo Awai skinned the chief
Like a wild beast;
The leaves of the olwedo tree,
He was covered by the leaves of the
  olwedo tree;
Spears clashed with spears,
In vain he invoked his luck;
In the battle led by Lengamoi,
The warriors of Patongo were
  burnt in the fire
Like wild beasts.

77

| Agoro opong i Langwen | *The army of Agoro has filled the valley of Langwen* |

Ee, Agoro opong i Langwen ye,

Gem konya ki mogo;

Nen lweny ki joni tek;
Omera ringo tong Lango do,

Walamoi dwoka paco;
Lweny ki Lango tek macalo man,
Walaro Nyamukina;
Agoro opong i Langwen.

The army of Agoro has filled the valley of Langwen,

People of Gem, come, help me fight them.

Behold, fighting the Lango is not easy;
My brother flees from the spear of the Lango;

Walamoi, take me home,
Fighting the Lango is so difficult,
We flee towards Nyamukina;
The army of Agoro has filled the valley of Langwen.

78

Wulwong pol Ayago obin

Wulwong pol Ayago obin,
Jo Puranga mito nywarowa;
Olal ocamo dyang pa jo
Medo ki ronynyo jo;
Kayo wa ye,
Wulwong pol Ayago obin.

Call the warriors of Ayago together

Call the warriors of Ayago together,
The people of Puranga are insulting us;
Olal has eaten our cattle,
And now he affronts us;
This bites us painfully, oh,
Call the warriors of Ayago together.

79
Tongo gang oloya

Tongo gang oloya,
Kono adok wi obur ye?

Lweny ki Lango tek,
Lweny ki Lango oloya,
Kany ma adok kwene?
Rwot tin adok kwene?

*I have failed to establish a
home*
I have failed to establish a village,
*Perhaps I should return to the deserted
site;*
Fighting the Lango is difficult;
I have failed to fight the Lango.
Where shall I go now?
My chief, where shall I go now?

In omera we

In omera we,
Adeg lok anywar;
In iyelo lupaco;

In omera we,
Gwok ier ali,
Wang ca ma binni,
Dong kari ye;
Jalli onywaro lupaco,

In omera we,
Adeg lok kolo,
Gwok iyelo lupaco.

You, my brother, listen

You, my brother, listen,
I don't like your insults;
You bring trouble to people in their
    own homes;

You, my brother, listen,
Do not provoke us,
For in a short while
You will see trouble;
This man insults people in their own
    homes;

You, my brother, listen,
I don't like your provocations;
Do not trouble people in their own
    homes.

The Dirges

Ah! from what agonies of heart and brain
What exaltations trampling on despair
What tenderness, what tears, what hope of wrong,
What passionate outcry of a soul in pain
Uprose this poem of earth and air.

Henry Longfellow: *Divina Commedia*

When you were on earth
I shared all with you equally.
Now I claim in death no less to share
a grave with you

Sophocles: *Electra*

There is no greater pain
than to recall a happy time
in wretchedness.

Dante: *Inferno*

81

Awinyo bila pa meya	*I heard the horn of my love*
Awinyo bila pa meya,	*I heard the horn of my love,*
Oto Cura koni bino,	*Oto Cura will soon come,*
Bila pare okok odiko con.	*His horn sounded early in the morning.*
Omera, angiyo kwe	*But I search for my brother in vain*
Ki i wanga yo do!	*Along the pathway, oh!*
Ah, Cura koni oo,	*Ah, Cura will soon be here,*
Bila pare okok odiko con.	*His horn sounded early in the morning.*

Omera kodo ma yamo

Omera kodo ma yamo,
Deg bino do!
En acel,
Gin pa maa yo!
Omera kodo ma yamo.
Wi-lobo obalo rwot awobe woko!

Akuru ki i yo kwe,
Deg bino ada!

My brother blows like the wind

My brother blows like the wind,
He refuses to come back, oh!
The only one,
Beloved of my mother, oh!
My brother blows like the wind.
Fate has destroyed the chief of youths,
    oh!

In vain I wait on the pathway,
He utterly refuses to come back.

83
Gira woto mubolo adyany

Gira woto mubolo adyany;

Canna do,
Can omoto i koma;
Nyodo ger
Ugol woko ye!
Anok wai ocito
I lugot,
Gira woto mubolo adyany.

*My daughter's buttocks dance
    as she walks*

*My daughter's buttocks dance as she
    walks.*
My sorrows, oh,
Sorrow has sunk deep into my flesh;
Daughter of the brave,
Dig her out of the grave oh!
But Anok has gone to her man
In the hills.
*My daughter's buttocks dance as she
    walks.*

84

Myel opong loka ca	*There is a big dance yonder*

Myel opong loka ca,
Orobo tye Cua,
Orobo Aming otoro komgi:

    Anga ma neno kono pa meya?

    Anga ma winyo bila pa meya?

    Anga ma ngeyo wer pa meya?
    Anga ma winyo bul pa meya?

Orobo tye Cua,
Orobo Aming otoro komgi;

    Maa, Okoya angiyo kwe!

There is a big dance yonder,
The youths of our clan are at Cua,
The youths of Aming are gathered together.

    But who can spot the headdress of love?

    Who can hear the sound of the horn of my love?

    Who knows the song of my love?
    Do you hear the drumming of my love?

The young men of our clan are at Cua,
The youths of Aming are gathered together,

    But, mother, I have searched for Okoya in vain!

85

Oteka lwenyo kene	*The warrior fights alone*
Oteka lwenyo kene,	*The warrior fights alone,*
Twon kara to kene ada!	*Behold the bull dies alone oh!*
Abong kony omeru ba;	*Abong, why, help your brother;*
En acel to woko do!	*The only one, he is dying, oh!*
Obalo ngo pa jo pa Awic?	*What wrong has he done to the children of Awic?*
Omera lwenyo kene?	*Why should my brother fight death alone?*

Omera lwenyo ki atero balibali

Omera lwenyo ki atero balibali,

Lwenyo bongo omin;

Tin oweko paco
Odong ma lik, ada;
Awodi lakony kore peke.
Bedo onyo lubedo kenikeni,
kakony kore peke.
Omera lwenyo ki atero biri,

Lwenyo ki bur.

My brother fights with barbed-headed arrows

My brother fights with barbed-headed arrows,

He fights single-handed, no brother beside him.

Today he has left the homestead,
And it is awful;
The young man fought single-handed.
Today, men live separately, no brother beside him;
My brother fought with barbed-headed arrows,
He fought with the grave.

87

Wod maa olwenyo ki too kwe	*Son of my mother has fought unsuccessfully with death*

Wod maa olwenyo ki too kwe,

Son of my mother has fought unsuccessfully with death,

Too dong ongayo wang lapyem,
Obalo gira kicol ye;

Death has defeated the boastful one,
It has destroyed my own, the one with the dark skin;

Latin, lakony kore peke
Ki kin omege.
To oneko lagingi,
To oniko omera ma yam ageno.
Omera dong olwenyo ki too kwe,

My brother fought single-handed,
No help from his brothers.
Death has killed the insistent one,
Has killed the brother whom I trusted.
My brother fought unsuccessfully with death,

To dong balo lapyem ye,
Oneko omera kicol ye;

It has destroyed the boastful one,
Has killed my own, the one with the dark skin;

Laco, kwany raifol,
Icel too,
To oneko lagingi,
To otero omera ma yam ageno.

Man, take a rifle,
Shoot death.
Death has killed the insistent one,
Has taken my brother whom I trusted.

88

Mac owang Layima	*Fire rages at Layima*

Mac owang Layima ye,
Mac owang kulu Cumu,
Owango nginyinginyi woko;
Kono ao pa min too,

Nyara, kono ariyo raa ma bor,

Kono ao pa min too,

Kono awango nginyinginyi woko;

Mac owang kulu Cumu ye.

Owang Layima ye,
Mac owang kulu Cumu,
Owango nginyinginyinginyi;
Kono ao pa min too,

Lutua, maku lweny ma tek,

Kono ao pa min too,

Kono awango nginyinginyi woko,

Mac owang kulu Cumu ye.

Fire rages at Layima, oh,
Fire rages in the valley of River Cumu,
Everything is utterly utterly destroyed;
If I could reach the homestead of death's mother,

My daughter, I would make a long grass torch;

If I could reach the homestead of death's mother,

I would destroy everything utterly utterly,

Like the fire that rages in the valley of River Cumu.

It rages at Layima, oh,
Fire rages in the valley of River Cumu,
Everything is utterly utterly destroyed;
If I could reach the homestead of Death's mother,

My clansmen, we would fight ruthlessly,

If I could reach the homestead of death's mother,

I would destroy everything utterly utterly,

Like the fire that rages in the valley of River Cumu.

Gin pa maa calo dek angweda

Gin pa maa calo dek angweda;

Oyaro wange,
Lake nyim oro.

Obalo nyodo her,
Tin olal woko,
Latin ker,
Gin pa maa
Calo dek angweda.

Beloved of my mother is like plucked vegetable leaves

*Beloved of my mother
  is like plucked vegetable leaves;*

His large eyes are wide open,
*His teeth are white like dry-season
  simsim;*

Death has destroyed a prince,
Today, he is lost.
Son of the chief,
Beloved of my mother
Is like plucked vegetable leaves.

90

Tong raa	*The hippopotamus spear*

Tong raa koyo oneko ye;
Abila pa wora opito an do,

Ee, kitino tua,
Abila pa wora opito an;

Mukumoi ye,
Twon dano pa aba;
Joni weko tong butu ki koyo;

Joni oweko tong raa butu woko.

Tong raa nyal ocamo ye;

Kitino pa wora okwero an woko;

Ee, kitino wa,
Abila pa wora okwero an do,

Mukumoi ye,
Twon dano pa aba,
Wun uweko tong butu ataa,

Joni oweko tong raa butu woko,

Tong raa ngom omayo ye.

The hippopotamus spear feels cold, oh;
This is the shrine of my father
that has fed me,

You, my clansmen,
This is the shrine of my father
that has fed me;

Mukumoi, oh,
Bull of men, son of my father;
The people have left the hippopotamus
spear in the cold;

They have left the hippopotamus spear
to sleep outside.

The hippopotamus spear has been
eaten by rust;

The children of my father have
rejected me;

You, my clansmen,
The shrine of my father has rejected me
oh;

Mukumoi, oh,
Bull of men, son of my father,
You have left the spear in the wrong
place,

They have left the hippopotamus spear
to sleep outside,

The hippopotamus spear was snatched
by the earth, oh!

Kwac pa maa	*Leopard of my mother*
Kwac pa maa yo,	*Leopard of my mother, oh;*
Gira bako doge;	*My own, he pleaded,*
Okutu bila ki i olet.	*He blew his horn in the pastures.*
Joni oneno i dyel rac;	*They have read the entrails of a goat, it is bad.*
Gira koko kore,	*My own, he cried with pain in his chest,*
Kome lit;	*His body was painful;*
Omwoco te Larumu.	*He shouted his praise-name at the foot of Larumu hill.*

92

Too owango kom anyaka	*Death burned the body of the young woman*
Too owango kom anyaka,	*Death burned the body of the young woman,*
Wango ma mac;	*Like fire,*
Anyaka koko kore,	*She cried with pain in her chest,*
Gin pa maa, yo;	*Beloved of my mother, oh;*
To wango komi,	*Death burned your body,*
Tin olo oteri.	*At last, today, it has taken you.*

93

En acel loo woko	*The only son of my mother has melted away*
En acel loo woko do;	*The only son of my mother has melted away, oh;*
Omera kutu kiliko ye;	*My brother used to blow his flute;*
Twon co wa dong peke.	*Our bull of men is no more.*
Nyodo Alal okutu bila,	*Son of Alal blew his horn,*
Ineno nyodo pa Alal	*Son of Alal used to blow his horn,*
Yam okutu bila wi jobi;	*Ee, he blew his horn standing atop the buffalo that he had killed;*
Omera kutu wi laro ye;	*My brother used to blow his horn from the hill top, oh.*
Ee, en acel loo woko do!	*The only son of my mother has melted away, oh!*

94

Anyongo wi yat	*I am squatting on a tree*
Anyongo wi yat	*I am squatting on a tree*
Calo winyo;	*Like a bird;*
An calo ayom	*I am like a monkey*
Munyongo wi yat.	*Squatting on a tree.*
Ai, maa,	*Oh, mother,*
Wi-lobo ogungu koma;	*Fate has knelt on me;*
An awac ango?	*What can I say?*
Ee, wi-lobo gungu koma;	*Ee, fate has crushed me completely;*
Can omoto i koma, ee!	*Suffering has sunk deeply in my flesh, ee!*

95

Woko okelo ayela

Woko okelo ayela,
Gin pa maa,
Wod pa Labwor,
Woko obolla dwongo;

Can man ocako ayela
Ma pud atin,
Bedo wi lobo,
Ocako gire ma yamu, do!
Piny man otima rac, ada,
Latin pa abaa,
Nyodo pa Labwor,
Woko otingnga dwongo;

Ee, woko okelo ayela
Wa ka-latin,
Bedo wi lobo;
Okwongo gire ki lalute ye!

Fate has brought troubles

Fate has brought troubles,
Beloved of my mother,
Son of Labwor,
Fate has thrown me the largest basket
*   to fill with dead children!*

My sufferings began
When I was only a child;
The troubles of this world,
It all began as a joke, oh!
This world has treated me badly,
Child of my father,
Son of Labwor,
Fate has thrown me the largest basket
*   to fill with dead children!*

Ee, fate began to trouble me
When I was only a child;
The sufferings of this world,
Fate first threw me the smallest basket
*   to fill with dead children!*

96

Kipwola ocaka con	*My troubles began long ago*

Kipwola ocaka con,
Ki i maa;

Wi-lobo, an aoro me pa nga?
Ee, wi-lobo, an aoro me pa nga?

Owiny ma nyodo oloyo,
Owiny, omera,
Nyodo calo mito loyi, do;

Ee, kipwola ocaka con
Ki i maa!

My troubles began long ago,
When I was still in my mother's
    womb;

Fate, tell me, whose child shall I send?
Ee, whose child shall I send
    to fetch me things?

Owiny has failed to get a child,
Owiny, my brother,
You seem to have failed to get a
    child, oh;

Ee, my troubles began long ago,
When I was still in my mother's womb!

97

Ai maa	*Oh mother*
Ai maa,	*Oh mother,*
Liwota ling doga,	*My love does not speak to me,*
Pingo ka?	*Why, oh?*
Omera ling doga,	*My love does not speak to me,*
Can dyang balo remo.	*Poverty in cattle has ruined my love;*
Can dyang ki remo ye,	*Poverty in cattle, my love, oh;*
Lamoo tino.	*Oil of my youth,*
Ee, omera ka ito,	*Ee, my brother, if you are dead,*
Opwoyo luyikwa weng!	*Let them bury both of us!*

Ceng pud bedo gikwed cware atena	*She used to sit close to her husband*
Ceng pud bedo	*She used to sit*
Gikwed cware atena;	*Close to her husband, touching each other;*
Laber pa min Amoo,	*The beautiful one, sister of Amoo,*
Anyaka wakke ya en aye.	*She used to boast, the one loved most by her husband;*
Okwanyo can ma i koma weng;	*He had removed all her worries completely.*
Latin wi-lobo ogungu kome.	*Fate has knelt on her*
Ai maa,	*Oh mother,*
Wi-lobo ogungu kome ye;	*Fate has crushed her completely.*
Ceng pud bedo gikwed cware atena.	*She used to sit close by her husband, touching each other!*

99

Ee, waya	*Ee, my aunt*
Ee, waya,	*Ee, my aunt,*
To pa lacan too atura;	*The death of the poor is sudden;*
Waya kideyo adeya kono?	*My aunt, was she strangled?*
Too ango muneko waya,	*What death has killed my aunt?*
Lacan otoo nget yo;	*The poor woman died on the roadside;*
Lacan otoo atura,	*The poor thing died suddenly;*
Nga mudeye kono?	*Who has strangled my aunt?*
To pa lacan too atura.	*The death of the poor is sudden.*
Ai maa,	*Oh, mother,*
Awinyo ki ngwece do!	*I heard her by her smell oh,*
Too pa lacan too atura;	*The death of the poor is sudden;*
Awinyo ki ngwece nget gudu;	*I heard her by her smell on the roadside;*
Twol ango mukayo waya?	*What snake bit my aunt?*
Lacan otoo nget yo;	*The poor woman died on the roadside;*
Lacan otoo atura,	*The poor thing died suddenly;*
Ngu mukaye kono?	*Was she killed by a lion?*
Too pa lacan too atura.	*The death of the poor is sudden.*
Ee, malaya,	*Ee, harlot;*
To pa lacan too atura;	*The death of the poor is sudden;*
Ee, malaya lugero agera,	*Ee, harlot, somebody slept with her,*
Twon nyac muneko waya?	*Perhaps a bull syphilis killed my aunt?*
Wayagi too ataa ataa;	*My aunt has died a foolish death;*
Lacan otoo atura,	*The poor thing died suddenly;*
Nga muneke kono?	*Who killed her?*
Too pa lacan too atura.	*The death of the poor is sudden.*

Lajok otoo ber

Lajok otoo ber,
In Ulula, in Ulula,
Bong cune ka dong okwee;

Jal man myelo ki kiniga,
Bong cune ka dong okwee;

Nyer man myelo myel ki kolo;
Ee, lajok otoo ber, in Ulula.

The witch is dead, and it is good news

The witch is dead, and it is good news;
Ulula, you, you Ulula,
*Touch his penis, see if it is cold and
    soft;*

Why, this man dances with anger;
*Touch his penis, see if it is cold and
    soft;*

Look, this man dances with fury.
*Ee, the witch is dead, and it is good
    news.*

Lukaka nyeru mono tunu

My clansmen, you may laugh awhile

Ee, lukaka, nyeru mono tunu,

Ee, my clansmen, you may laugh awhile,

Kadi ubedo li-kiny-kiny,
Lukaka, nyeru mono tunu;
Kodi too muneka ni,
Mwaka maka bino ki wun ba,
Kadi wubedo li-kiny-kiny,
Lukaka nyeru mono tunu.

I see you shaking with laughter,
My clansmen, you may laugh awhile;
This death that has killed my beloved,
May visit you next year;
I see you shaking with laughter,
My clansmen, you may laugh awhile.

Too oneko min liwota woko

Too oneko min liwota woko ye,
Wadoko ma rom;
Ee, lakare ber,
Waum auma.
Dong waloko kwed anga?
Acel long ma yam ageno.
Dong warom.
Too oneko min liwota woko,
Koni wadoko ma rom.

Death has killed my friend's mother

Death has killed my friend's mother oh,
Now we are equal;
Ee, this man of good fortune,
Let us celebrate it.
With whom shall I speak now?
She was the only one I trusted.
Now we are equal.
Death has killed my friend's mother,
Now we are equal.

Odur, kan kana woko

Odur, kan kana woko,
Kana odong ki litino alima,
Odur, kana dong ki mon;
Litino alima oleyo gang pa Kao;

Paco odong ki alima ye,
Ee, Odur we,
Odur kan lim woko,
Lim odong ki litino alima,
Odur, lonyo dong ki mon;
Litino alima oleyo gang pa joni,

Paco odong ki alima.

Odur, hide the donkeys
somewhere

Odur, hide the donkeys somewhere,
They will be inherited by slaves,
Odur, the women will take the donkeys :
Slaves have taken over the homestead
of Kao,
The home now belongs to slaves;
Ee, Odur, listen,
Hide the donkeys somewhere,
The wealth will remain for slaves,
Odur, the women will take the wealth;
Slaves have taken over the homestead
of those people;
The home now belongs to slaves.

Otenyo lonyo ki la-laku

Otenyo lonyo ki la-laku, do yo,

Ee, laber pa Amoo
Yam otenyo lonyo;
Oweko dyang ki la-laku do,
La-laku wakke kwede,
Owedko lim ma cwinya cwer;
Jalli otenyo lonyo kulu ki wegi,
Ineno la-laku wai kome gum!

Oweko bati ki la-laku, doyo,

Ye, latin pa Amoo
  yam iye yom;
Otenyo lela ki la-laku do,
Jalli wakke nono,
Onongo lonyo ki bot oworo;
Jalli oweko lim kulu ki wegi,
Mye, la-laku wai kome gum.

*He has left his wealth to the
  inheritor*

*He has left all his wealth to the
  inheritor, oh;*
Ee, the beautiful son of Amoo
Left all his wealth;
He left the cattle to the inheritor,
Now the inheritor boasts with them;
He left all his wealth, I am so sad;
The man left all his wealth to others,
What a lucky inheritor!

*He left his iron-roofed house to the
  inheritor,*
Ee, the son of Amoo was most generous;

He left his bicycle to the inheritor, oh,
This man boasts for nothing,
He got all the wealth from the dead.
He left all his wealth for the inheritor,
Ha, this inheritor is most lucky.

Ceng ma too peke

Ceng ma too peke,
La-laku lako gin ango?
Dyang odong ki la-laku do;

Ee, la-laku nongo ngo?
Baki odong ki la-laku do;

Ee, ceng ma too peke,
La-laku lony kwene ka?
Lela odong ki la-laku do;

La-laku man kome gum;
Nye, omera, in mono,
Ceng ma too peke,
La-rac, inyomo nya pa anga?

Dako odong ki la-laku do;
Ee, la-laku kwo kanye?

Ot odong ki la-laku do;

Ceng ma too peke,
La-laku lako gon ango?

If death were not there

If death were not there,
Where would the inheritor get things?
The cattle have been left for the inheritor;

Ee, how would the inheritor get things?
The iron-roofed house has been left for the inheritor;

Ee, if death were not there,
How would the inheritor get rich?
The bicycle has been left for the inheritor;

This inheritor is most lucky;
Ee, brother, tell me,
If death were not there,
Ugly one, whose daughter would have married you?

A wife has been left for the inheritor;
Ee, inheritor, how would you have lived?

The house has been left for the inheritor;

If death were not there,
How would the inheritor get things?

PART III

Themes in Acoli Dirges

The Acoli dirges fall into six movements or themes, which embody the six ways in which the Acoli people react to the crisis of death: (*a*) Songs of the pathway; (*b*) Songs of the battle with Death:(*c*) Songs of surrender; (*d*) Songs of cruel fate; (*e*) The attack on the dead; and (*f*) The attack on the living.

(a) *Songs of the pathway*

These poems are characterised by a kind of ambivalence as to whether the dead one is really gone for ever. As in the love songs, the mourner refuses to believe that the one he or she loved so much is no more; and so she sings:

> I heard the horn of my love,
> Oto Cura will soon come,
> His horn sounded early in the morning . . .

She scans the crowd in search of her dead lover:

> There is a big dance yonder,
> Who can spot the headdress of my love?
> Who can hear the sound of the horn of my love?
> Do you hear the drumming of my love?

The mother of a dead young woman tells us that she is not really dead, but:

> Anok has gone to her man
> In the hills . . .

Gerald Moore has suggested[1] that this ambivalence helps to adjust to the shock and grief of the living, since it puts off the moment when the finality of personal death must be recognised. But, as we have seen, the funeral dance is held many months after death has occurred. These poems, instead of postponing the moment when the finality of death must be faced, actually rake up the bitter memory of the tragedy. And, in fact, each one contains the recognition that the dead one has gone for ever. Thus, after telling us that Oto Cura will soon come, because his horn was heard in the morning, the mourner adds:

[1] 'The imagery of death in African poetry', *Africa*, Vol. 38, 1968, p. 68.

> But I search for my brother in vain
> Along the pathway.

And, of Anok who had just gone to her man in the hills, we are asked to

> Dig her out of the grave, oh!

The Dama sing:

> You, full-breasted one, have died,
> Arise and grasp your stick,
> Let us go out together to dig out the fieldmouse.
> Are you truly dead?
> Do you live, and yet lie there?
> Arise, cut a stick and let us go to look for the fieldmouse.

Commenting on this poem, Bowra stated, 'They (the primitives) often exploit the pathetic fancy that the dead person must arise and return to the usual tasks . . .'[2] But this theme of ambivalence is also found in Western literature. The best example is Walt Whitman's 'O Captain! My Captain!':

> O Captain! my Captain! our fearful trip is done,
> The ship has weather'd every rack, the prize we sought is won,
> The port is near, the bells I hear, the people all exulting . . .
>> But O heart! heart! heart!
>> O the bleeding drops of red!
>>> Where on the deck my Captain lies,
>>> Fallen cold and dead.

> O Captain! my Captain! rise up and hear the bells;
> Rise up—for you the flag is flung—for you the bugle trills,
> For you bouquets and ribbon'd wreaths—for you the shores crowding,
> For you they call, the swaying mass, their eager faces turning; . . .

> My Captain does not answer, his lips are pale and still,
> My father does not feel my arm, he has no pulse nor will . . .
>> Exult O shores! and sing O bells!
>> But I, with mournful tread,
>>> Walk the deck my Captain lies,
>>> Fallen cold and dead.

[2] C. M. Bowra, *Primitive Song*, a Mentor Book, 1963, p. 96.

The poems in this category capture that moment of disbelief which is displayed when the news of the death of a beloved one hits one like a meteorite. The first reaction is not so much of shock or frustration, but of disbelief. How can a person so young, so beautiful, so vigorous and so wonderful actually die? It is inconceivable. It must be a joke. Did I not hear his horn in the morning? Did we not all see her going to her man in the hills? Indeed, the news is often met with a laugh or a giggle. Shock and despair follow soon afterwards.

Paul Valery[3] said the following at the burial of his bosom friend Pierre Louys: 'Yesterday, under the great impact of a few words, it seemed as though a huge fragment of life had fallen away from me, uncovering some great gaping, smarting wound, where hundreds of memories appeared suddenly exposed and, as though maddened by the sudden light of death, rushing in unimaginable disorder, as if trying to repair the loss suffered by my heart and grasping desperately at the past. In the place of the unthinkable event, there came this swarm of memories which would not accept the fact of death.'[4]

During the funeral dance, the Acoli relive this terrible moment of hopeless and pathetic disbelief, as captured in these songs of the pathway. The Acoli do not make statues of their heroes and lovers; and the grave mound soon disappears. The memory of the beloved is locked in such dirges.

(b) *Songs of the battle with Death*

In these dirges we see the dying man locked in a fierce feud with Death, watched, as it were, by his loved ones, who are utterly helpless, and cannot do anything to save him. During illness, of course, the relatives do all they can to fight the causes of ill-health. A diviner is consulted, and her prescriptions are administered swiftly and as accurately as possible. A hostile spirit is exorcised and driven away or pacified; the patient is nursed with loving care. But in death there is nothing more that the living can do.

The Russian poet Yevgeny Yevtushenko has expressed the same hopeless situation in his poem 'Don't die, Ivan Stepanych':[5]

[3] *Masters and Friends*, trans. Martin Turnell, New York, 1968, p. 284.
[4] Sir Arthur Quiller-Couch, ed., *Oxford Book of English Verse*, new edition, 1955, p. 899.
[5] *Bratsk Station and other poems*, trans. Tina Tupikina-Glaessner, Godfrey Dutton and Igor Mezhakoff-Koriakin, New York, 1967, pp. 125–7.

Don't die, don't die
It is wrong to act like this
Forsaking your paternal land.
You lie there in Bratsk city hospital . . . and all around you are nurses,
    syringes, and whiteness . . .
You are surrounded with kindness and attention but you are departing . . .
Doctors, I beg you, help him, do try and rouse him again . . .
Conqueror of Berlin
Can't you conquer death?

Acoli mourners tease each other about the whole pathetic predicament:

> The warrior fights alone,
> Behold the bull dies alone oh,
> Abong, why, help your brother . . .
> What wrong has he done to the children of Awic
> That he should die alone?

or:

> My brother fights with barbed-headed arrows;
> He fights alone, no brother beside him . . .

But, at long last, when they can no longer contain themselves, the
mourners burst out with a terrible cry:

> If I could reach the homestead of Death's mother,
> I would make a long grass torch;
> If I could reach the homestead of Death's mother,
> I would destroy everything utterly, utterly,
> Like the fire that rages at Layima,
> Like the fire that rages in the valley of River Cumu!

The Acoli mourner desires to visit the homestead of Death's mother,
and wreak vengeance. The Acoli do not appeal to a god or some other
power to intervene in their gravest crisis of life. They do not believe
that the death of a brother, father, mother, husband or wife is the wish
or will of some creator, to be accepted without question. This irre-
ligious stance of the Acoli contrasts vividly with the outlook of the
Nilotic Nuer who call themselves mere ants before their deity Kwoth.
When a child dies, the Nuer say Kwoth has taken what is his own and
human beings should not complain. 'If you grieve overmuch, God will
be angry that you should resent his taking what is his own.'[6]

[6] E. E. Evans-Pritchard, *Nuer Religion*, Oxford, 1965, p. 13.

Likewise, in Christian belief, the departed hopefully go to a desirable place called heaven. A funeral ceremony is seen as a farewell party for the ghost of the dead person. As Backman put it, '. . . . one should not sorrow at the departure of a human being but rather celebrate the day as one of joy and as a real birthday—of everlasting life in heavenly bliss.'[7]

This comforting approach to the crisis of death has produced a comforting type of death poetry. Hemans's 'Dirge'[8] goes:

> Calm on the bosom of God,
> Fair spirit, rest thee now!
> E'en while with thy footsteps trod,
> His seal was on thy brow.
> Dust to its narrow house beneath!
> Soul, to its place on high!
> They that have seen thy look in death
> No more may fear to die.

And John Donne[9] scorns death as follows:

> Death, be not proud, though some have callèd thee
> Mighty and dreadful, for thou art not so:
> For those whom thou think'st thou dost overthrow
> Die not, poor Death; not yet canst thou kill me . . .
>   . . . Why swell'st thou then?
> One short sleep past, we wake eternally,
> And Death shall be no more: Death, thou shalt die!

(c) *Songs of surrender*

In this movement, the clashes of battle in the songs above give way to quiet surrender. There is no fury, no accusations, no teasing; only acceptance of the naked fact of death. The physical pain suffered by the dead person at the last moments of his life, as well as the hopelessness of the case at the deathbed, are recalled and celebrated.

> Son of my mother has fought unsuccessfuly with Death,
> Death has defeated the boastful one,
> It has destroyed my own, the one with the dark skin . . .

[7] E. Louis Backman, *Religious dances in the Christian church and popular medicine*, trans. E. Classen, London, 1952, p. 140.

[8] Felicia Dorothea Hemans, in *Oxford Book of English Verse*, p. 735.

[9] *Oxford Book of English Verse*, p. 238.

or:

> They have read the entrails of a goat,
> It is bad.
> My own, he cried with pain in his chest,
> His body was painful.

or:

> Death burns the body of the woman
> Like fire . . .
> Beloved of my mother oh,
> Death burned your body;
> At last, today it has taken you.

This theme of surrender is found in the Chinese poet Su Tung P'o,[10] when he cried:

> I will never be able to stop my tears.
> And the day is far off when I will
> Forget this cruel day . . .
> I was warned of it in a dream.
> No medicine would have helped,
> Even if it had been heaped mountain high . . .

And in the Dhammapada[11] we read:

> Death comes and carries off that man
> absorbed in his children and flocks . . .
> Sons are no help, nor father, nor relations;
> There is no help from kinship for the one
> whom death has seized.

In these songs the Acoli poets study the delicate nature of human life; they compare man to plucked vegetable leaves that soon wither and dry up, or the dew that vanishes soon after sunrise.

> Beloved of my mother
> Is like plucked vegetable leaves;
> His eyes are wide open,
> His teeth are like dry-season simsim;
> Death has destroyed a prince . . .

[10] *A hundred poems of the Chinese*, trans. Kenneth Roxroth, New York, 1965, p. 69.
[11] *Dhammapada* trans. Irving Babbitt, New York, 1936, p. 44.

or:

> The only son of my mother has melted away oh!
> My brother used to blow his flute;
> Our bull of men is no more . . .

One of the Goliard poets, possibly Peter Abelard, used similar images: [12]

> Mourn then the flower
> Plucked, faded, festering;
> Bright but an hour
> Like a star a-westering . . .

These poems take us back to the side of the deathbed, where the relatives are sitting, watching in silence. We hear the groans of the dying man, and occasionally cast our minds back and see the man in the prime of his life, in full battle-dress, or in the dancing arena; we hear his horn after a successful hunt or in the pastures. The fact of death is accepted calmly as they watch the candle of life being blown out.

(d) *Songs of cruel fate*

In these poems the poets survey the plight of the living, the individuals who are left to suffer, the men and women who continue to feel distress, frustration, anger, despair, and sorrow as a result of the death of a beloved one. Fate kneels on people and crushes them completely. 'Kneeling and crushing' are hunting images. When a buffalo is critically wounded, so that it has no more strength to charge with its horns, it tries to fall on its adversary, and kill him with its massive weight.

The words *woko*, *wi-lobo*, and *ru-piny*,[13] which I have interpreted here as fate, actually mean the human predicament; they represent the suffering, risks, problems and challenges that the individual faces during his or her lifetime. Against them, man is impotent. They kneel on man and crush him completely. In this world man is like a bird or a monkey squatting on a tree; he is the target of the troubles of this world.

[12] *The Goliard Poems: Medieval Latin Songs and Satires*, trans. G. F. Whicher, New York, 1949, pp. 69–71.
[13] For a detailed study see Okot p'Bitek, *Religion of the Central Luo*, Nairobi, 1971, Chapter 9.

> I am squatting on a tree
> Like a bird,
> I am like a monkey
> Squatting on a tree;
> Oh mother,
> Fate has knelt on me . ...

A man who has lost a number of children speaks of fate having thrown him the largest basket, *dwongo*, to fill with dead children, before any would live:

> Fate has brought troubles,
> Beloved of my mother,
> Son of Labwor,
> Fate has thrown me the largest basket
> To fill with dead children . . .
> It all began as a joke, oh!
> This world has treated me badly . . .

There is nothing that man can do to prevent fate carrying out its cruel schemes. Cruel as they are, *woko*, *wi-lobo*, and *ru-piny* are senseless, deaf and blind. No sacrifices are offered to them, because they are unreasonable; a prayer to them, or any argument would fall on stone walls. These are mere names of the sum total of human sufferings and the misfortunes of Man.

Su Tung P'o sang:[14]

> Why should I not have died with him?
> His clothes still hang on the rack.
> His milk is still by his bed.
> Overcome, it is as though life had left us.
> We lie prostrate and insensible all day . . .

The Acoli mourner pleads with her dead beloved:

> Brother, why do you not speak to me?
> Brother, if you are dead,
> Let them bury both of us.

Whatever might have been the immediate cause of the misfortune, at this stage, the Acoli take it to mean an attack of fate on the living individual. These poems are not about the dead; they celebrate the

[14] *A hundred poems of the Chinese*, p. 69

sufferings of the living. The funeral dance provides the opportunity for self-contemplation; the picture of Man's suffering is portrayed in these terrible songs of cruel fate.

(e) *The attack on the dead*

The body of the dead person is always treated with great respect and fear, and the burial rites are conducted with dignity and restraint. But in this group of songs the Acoli turn upon the dead with a viciousness which is not easy to explain. A dead aunt is accused of being a harlot, and the poet wonders whether she was not killed by syphilis. Now, an aunt, that is, one's father's sister, is a most respected person. As soon as one has succeeded in winning a girl, the token of love that is given to him by the girl is always taken to the aunt, who sets the machinery of the marriage in motion. No one ever insults his aunt. But in this song the poet uses the most unseemly expressions and words to describe the death of the aunt:

> Ee, harlot,
> The death of the poor is sudden;
> Ee, harlot, somebody slept with her,
> My aunt has died a foolish death;
> The poor thing died suddenly . . .

Another dead woman is accused of having ruined the homestead and is described as a 'nobody'. One dead man is called a witch, and the mourners declare that it is good that he is dead.

Gerald Moore has commented on the first song as follows, 'Here the singer curiously alternated expressions of genuine compassion at the sad and anonymous nature of the poor woman's death with expressions of scorn and anger at the disgrace she had brought to her relations, both by the manner of the whore's life and her beggar-woman's death.' He interpreted this song in terms of what he called the African concept of 'praise', which, according to him, 'includes the enumeration of the dead man's faults and failures as well as his virtues. The poet gathers up all the complex of emotions aroused by the death of the woman. He does not reject any of them, whether it be sorrow at the friendlessness of her end, or the almost savage glee in speculating on her case. In this way, the total significance of her death is adjusted and placed within society.'[15]

[15] Op. cit., p. 67

Whatever the African concept of 'praise' is, these poems are certainly not meant to be praises; they are a direct attack on the dead, for the bad things they did while alive; even if one of these things is the act of dying. It is a great shame to have a relative who is a whore; it is a greater shame if that person is one's father's sister. A witch is an enemy of society; his death removes a dangerous man from society; people rejoice at his exit:

> The witch is dead;
> It is good that he is dead.
> You, Ulula,
> Touch his penis,
> See if it is cold and soft . . .
> Ee, the witch is dead, and it is good news.

It is this anger and disgust against the dead which forms the core of the song of the Hungarian poet Attila József in which he attacks his dead mother.[16]

> Mother, my fever is a hundred and six, and you aren't here to take care of me. Instead, like an easy woman, you just lay by death's side as soon as he signalled you . . .
> You are worthless! You just want to be dead!
> You spoil everything! You are a ghost!
> You are a greater cheat than any woman,
> Who deceived me and led me on . . .
> O you gypsy, you wheeled, you gave,
> Only to steal it all back in the last hour.

In 'Young wind', Confucius compared a certain man with a rat, and in his opinion, the man was below the level of a rat.[17]

> A rat has a skin at least,
> But a man who is a mere beast
> Must also die,
> His death being an end of no decency.
> A rat has teeth,
> But this fellow, for all his size, is beneath
> the rat's level;
> Why delay his demise?

[16] 'Consciousness', translated by John Batki, mimeo.
[17] *The Confucian Odes*, ed. Ezra Pound, New York, 1954, p. 24.

It is the disappointment of the living that causes them to attack the dead. These poems, far from being 'praises', are actually social condemnation of the dead person.

(f) *The attack on the living*

In these songs the mourners completely forget the dead, forget their own sorrows, even forget the fact that they are related to one another, and hit out against one another. Instead of comforting a friend and a relative who has lost his mother, we hear:

> Death has killed my friend's mother, oh,
> Now we are equal;
> Ee, this man of good fortune,
> Let us celebrate it . . .

The inheritor, that is, one of the brothers who is chosen to take over the wife, children and property of the dead man, comes under heavy punishment. In one song, he is discriminated against and labelled a slave.

> Odur, hide the donkeys somewhere,
> They will be inherited by slaves,
> Odur, the women will take the donkeys:
> Slaves have taken over the homestead of Kao . . .

In the next poem, the inheritor is told not to boast since all the property he has, he got from the dead man:

> . . . He left his bicycle to the inheritor, oh,
> This man boasts for nothing,
> He got all his wealth from the dead.
> He left all his wealth for the inheritor,
> He, this inheritor is most lucky.

Blinded by jealousy, brothers sting one another with mean poems, and ask the inheritor, 'If death were not there, how would you get rich?'

> If death were not there,
> Where would the inheritor get things?
> The cattle have been left for the inheritor;
> Ee, where would the inheritor get things?

> . . . Ee, brother, tell me,
> If death were not there,
> Ugly one, whose daughter would have married you?
> A wife has been left for the inheritor . . .

As stated above, these attacks on brothers by brothers arise out of jealousies, the result of fierce competition among the eligible men for the favour of the widow, and the property of the dead man. To be chosen is a kind of vote of confidence; and as a result, the social status of the inheritor rises. But, they also embody social commentaries, and point out the weaknesses and failures of the inheritor.

Like the satirical attacks in the short stories exchanged around the evening fire, and the songs of bitter laughter found in this book, these poems do not cause social strife among the clansmen. On the contrary, they provide a channel through which members of this close-knit group pour out their grievances and jealousies against one another, in public. These attacks, with all the abuse, ridicule and cruel insults, act as a cleansing activity. The clan group that emerges from the funeral dance, which is the last of the ceremonies by which the crisis of death is faced, is a more strongly united and healthy social group.

Poets as Historians

Daniel E. Ongo has rightly described the songs of the Acoli people as 'Buk pa kwaariwa', 'The books of our ancestors'. He wrote, 'Our ancestors were very talented people . . . They recorded the wars they fought, the famines and other disasters such as droughts and other pestilences that befell them; they described the reigns of chiefs, praised their lovers, threw insults at their rivals and enemies, and sang of deaths they suffered . . . They knew that to talk about these things was not enough, for it is easy to forget spoken words, so they put these things into songs, so that they may not forget.'

In 1916 there was a fierce famine in East Acoli. The people of Pajule migrated to the western part of the country to seek succour. There was plenty of sweet potato in that area, and many lives were saved. When the famine was over, the chief of Pajule came to persuade his people to return home. A poet replied with this song:

Kong iciom ma i lalur,	*First, you go and fetch*
Ki ma olal i pii,	*Those entombed in the stomach of hyenas,*
Ka dok inyut dero bel,	*And those who perished in the river,*
Ka wek wadok malo;	*And then show us the millet granaries;*
Wan pud wabango lumone;	*Then we shall return to the east;*
Dero bel tye kwene?	*Where are the millet granaries?*

The song is historical, but only in a special sense. It is silent on a number of questions that an ordinary historian would ask. What was the cause of the famine? Did the entire Pajule people migrate to the west? Among which people did they stay? When did the Pajule ultimately return to their homes? How many people perished in the famine? and so on. But when elders meet, they discuss these very questions. The song plays a vital role in their discussions, because it is the core of the discussion. Indeed, the history of a chiefdom is usually reconstructed through the songs. Below are four such histories.

Bwobo
The people of Bwobo, who today number about two thousand, are found in Kilak and Omoro counties of Acoli District. Their history begins in Lango country. It is claimed that the branch which later

became the chiefly clan broke off from the main body of a southward-moving Luo group. For a time the group settled on Otuke hill; then, led by a man called Luo, they moved to Ngeta hill, near present-day Lira town. It was here that their leader Luo died, and was succeeded by Olum Panya. The following clan groups attached themselves to the group, and a chiefdom was founded: Lugwar, Lukoyo and Lami.

The young chiefdom experienced its first bitter war when the Lango clans of Alito and Pakwaca launched a combined attack and drove them out of Otuke, pursued them as far as Jabalu hill, and then routed them there again. Perhaps the oldest *otole* song of Bwobo commemorates this sad episode:

Tongo gang oloya,	*To establish a settlement I have failed;*
Kono adok wi obur ya?	*Or should I return to the site I deserted?*
Lweny ki Lango tek;	*Fighting the Lango is difficult;*
Lweny ki Lango oloya ye;	*I have failed to fight the Lango, oh,*
Kany ma adok kwene?	*Where shall I go now?*
Rwoda, tin adok kwene?	*My chief, where shall I go now?*

The shaken chiefdom returned and settled near Ngeta hill once again. Olum Panya was succeeded by Canya, who in turn was succeeded by Obwogo, whose name later became the name of the chiefdom. During Obwogo's rule a long drought struck, followed by a fierce famine. The people gathered together and went to the chief, urging him to do something about the suffering of the people. A diviner was consulted, and he prescribed that a leopard must be caught alive and sacrificed, then the rain would return and famine end.

Obwogo made an appeal to the clans to co-operate in the adventure. But he failed to enforce his will over the chiefdom. No leopard was caught, and the famine continued unabated. The following *bwola* song records the story: it blames the chief's weakness for the disobedience of the commoner clans, and accuses him of destroying the land. It tells of the loneliness of Obwogo, a chief without loyal subjects:

Ee, Obwogo mubalo paco;	*Ee, it is Obwogo who destroyed the settlement;*
Kadi icamo kwon,	*Although you eat millet bread,*
Makko kwac oloi ye;	*You have failed to catch a leopard;*
Ee, an do,	*Ee, oh, me, oh,*

An kena, Obwogo ye,	*I am alone, Obwogo oh,*
Lamiru kwero dog Luo ye,	*The commoner clans have rejected*
	the commands of the son of Luo, oh,
Kadi imato kongo,	*Although you drink beer,*
In keni Obwogo do,	*You are alone, Obwogo, oh,*
Obwogo mubalo paco!	*It is Obwogo who destroyed the*
	settlement.

Obwogo led his people across the Nile into Bunyoro to seek succour. When the famine was over the people demanded that they should return back home. The request was presented in the following *bwola* song, asking the chief to take them back to the land of their old chief Olum Panya, the hairy one.

Ee, alego rwoda ye,	*Ee, I ask my chief, oh,*
Ee, alego rwoda do,	*I ask my chief, oh,*
Tera bot Olum ma layer;	*Take me to Olum*
	the hairy one;
Ee, ka nenno Olum,	*Ee, to see Olum,*
Ma layer,	*The hairy one,*
Alego rwoda do,	*I ask my chief, oh,*
Tera bot Olum ma layer.	*Take me to Olum*
	the hairy one.

The request was granted, and Obwogo led his people back home. It was about this time that the chiefdom acquired the name Obwogo, which later became corrupted to Bwobo.

Obwogo was succeeded by Takar, and then came Lujibo whose rule is remembered because of floods that threatened the crops. Having consulted the diviner, Lujibo removed the rain stone, *kot amee*, from the cave in which it was normally kept and brought it outside, in the hope that the rains would then stop, and the floods subside. Indeed the rains stopped, and the crops were saved. But this was also the beginning of a long drought which resulted in a famine.

The chiefdom shrine had been founded on Omoro hill, and was, like many other chiefdom shrines, named after the hill. In the same way, the Jok, or deity of the Bwobo people is also called Omoro. The deity Omoro has a 'mother' named Ayugi, and a 'wife' known as Ayomo. Their two 'sons' are Bala and Kota. When the droughts raged, a poet composed the following prayer to the gods of

Bwobo to let the rains fall. According to the song, the causes of the drought were that the deities had become annoyed and had gone away. The poet invites them to return to Omoro hill.

Wac ki Kota oneko piny;	*Tell Kota he has destroyed the land;*
Wod Ayugi, dwog paco.	*Son of Ayugi, come home;*
Bala ma won piny,	*Bala, you owner of the land,*
Dwog paco,	*Come home;*
Wek kot ocwee;	*So that it may rain;*
Ka kot ocwee,	*When the rains fall,*
Kitino Omoro odwogo paco.	*The children of Omoro have come home.*

The next chief was appropriately called Ocieng—from *cieng*, sun. Then followed Abwor, and then Lagara. Lagara was killed in a hunting accident by a slave boy Kitot, who mistook the chief for a buffalo calf. Kitot was executed, despite the pleas of Lagara's mother, the queen mother. Whereupon, she made a curse on any person who would succeed her son. A succession crisis developed. Okutu Ayaru, brother of Lagara, declined the stool, and instead, broke away with his followers and moved away. The search for the successor of the royal stool continued. A delegation was sent across the Nile to Bunyoro, where, it was hoped, a male descendant of Obwogo might be found. When this hope was frustrated, a Munyoro youth was kidnapped and brought to Bwobo. They called him Ocaka-con, that is, 'misfortune began with me long ago'. Ocaka-con was put on the stool straightaway, although he was only a boy.

It appears that the new chief was not very healthy-looking; his skin had spots. A man from Dolo made some rude remarks about this fact. He was caught and punished by rubbing his mouth on the ground until it bled. The Dolo combined with Pakwaca and attacked Bwobo; but they were repulsed. In a counter-attack the settlements of the Dolo and Pakwaca were completely destroyed. A song arose from this victory:

Wumakka Dolo,	*Get me a man from Dolo,*
Kiree doge i ngom,	*Rub his mouth on the ground,*
Ka oyeto rwot;	*When he insults the chief;*
Ka guyeto rwot	*When they insult the chief,*
Wumakka Dolo,	*Get me the people of Dolo,*
Kiree doge i ngom.	*Rub their mouths on the ground.*

A new line of chiefs had been established. Latigo Abwo, who succeeded Ocaka-con, led his people to a new site on Okiga hill. He named it Atoo, 'I will die'; that is to say, should some enemy follow him there, he would fight to the death. There, the warriors of Bwobo engaged themselves in waylaying and killing 'foreigners' who passed by the hill, and many a man won battle titles, *nying moi*. One of the victims was probably a man from Payira. In 1902 the Payira attacked and burnt down a Bwobo village, and the following *otole* song was composed:

Alamo olweo ki jo Payira;	*I invoke my olwedo tree for the Payira;*
Lubwobo, luloka,	*Men of Bwobo, you Bantu,*
Miya woda;	*Give back my son.*
Tong okwongo poto	*The spear first struck*
Ki te Atoo;	*At the foot of Atoo hill;*
Bul kok kibuu ye;	*The drums sound at the foot of the kibuu tree, oh,*
Lubwobo loko laweewee, aiya.	*Men of Bwobo speak in whispers, o h.*

Latigo Abwo was succeeded by Otoo Aburu, who was retired by the British colonial authorities in 1916, and replaced by Muca Oryem. Oryem died the following year. In 1918 Bwobo was combined with Alero chiefdom and placed under Yocia Olwedo, chief of Alero. The new régime had arrived, and there ended the story of Bwobo chiefdom. A weak and small chiefdom, it had never possessed a chief strong enough to wield effective authority over the whole chiefdom. The allied commoner clans were seldom loyal, and some of them rebelled with impunity. The Bwobo were pushed hither and thither by more powerful groups. Their *bwola* and *otole* songs record the sad story faithfully. Their *mwoc*, praise-name, goes:

Ager ye,	*I am fierce, oh,*
Nguu ye,	*I am a wild beast, oh,*
Labwor ye,	*I am a lion, oh,*
Ka inyono yibe	*If you step on its tail*
Ci kayi;	*It bites you;*
Wang Kong ye!	*Wang Kong oh!*

Wang Kong is the name of the chiefly drum. This praise-name is in part a camouflage, a covering up of their fundamental weakness, by appearing and sounding fierce and strong like a lion; but, in part, it is also a sincere confession of their non-aggressive spirit, of the re-treating, battle-tired chiefdom. Latigo Abwo withdrew, as it were, to Okiga hill. He called it Atoo, 'Whoso follows me here, I will fight to the death'. The lion of Bwobo does not attack. It waits for you to tread on its tail, and then bites.

Palaro

The story of Bwobo chiefdom contrasts sharply with that of the aggress-ive, almost bloodthirsty people of Palaro, the small but warlike clans which loosely joined to form the chiefdom. Palaro had two chiefly drums; one was called Opimadur, and the other '*Bedo mot lukwero*', meaning, 'Living in peaceful co-existence is rejected'. Their tradition is silent as to when or where the eleven commoner clans associated with the chiefly clan.

Laro was the founder of the chiefly clan; he led his people across the Nile from Madi country, and settled on Lapul hill. From there they moved to Lute hill. These two landmarks play an important part in Palaro thinking. Lapul is the shrine of the chiefdom; and both Lapul and Lute appear in their *mwoc*, praise-name:

Lapul ye,	*Lapul oh,*
Lute ye,	*Lute oh,*
Lela ye,	*We are hard like ironstone,*
Lela Gelo ye;	*Like the ironstone at Gelo;*
Aneki nyong.	*I will kill you,*
	and who can avenge your death?

While on Lute hill, what might be called a conflict of customs pro-voked a crisis which led to a *coup d'état*. According to Palaro custom, when a girl or married woman was caught sleeping with a man, she paid the *luk*, fornication fine. Among other Acoli people the reverse was the case. Now, a girl was caught sleeping with the chief's son, and the chief demanded an exhorbitant *luk*, arguing that, after all, the young man was the chief's son, a very special person. The commoners did not like this, and there was much grumbling. When Obura, a Luo prince from Bunyoro, called at Lute, the Palaro gathered and put the case before him. Obura read the signs correctly and ruled that, from then on, men, and not women should pay the fine. At once the chief was destooled, and Obura installed in his place.

Obura met his death at the hands of Olum, another Luo prince from

Bunyoro. Olum attacked the Palaro with a large army, and the people climbed up the hill, which was immediately surrounded. The invaders began to dig around the hill, with the hope, it is said, of toppling it over. Though the attempt failed, the siege was long enough to starve the Palaro into surrender. Obura was executed by Olum, and Auya was made chief; but he was soon deposed, because he was a bad chief, and was replaced by Okelo. After Okelo, Lagero, Latigo and Kitara ruled the chiefdom. The last of the Palaro chiefs was Owor, who was removed from the chiefship by the District Commissioner Postlethwaite, who combined Palaro and Patiko, and made Lapir, chief of Patiko, head of the new unit.

As can be seen from the above, Palaro, as a chiefdom, was never a powerful force. In fact the different clans fought their own wars, almost independently. They fought numerous battles against neighbouring clans and chiefdoms: Padibe, Atyak, Parajok, Puranga, Payira, Koyo and Lukung. All these battles are recorded in the spear-songs of the different clans. This meant, in effect, that the Palaro could only field small fighting groups in any battle. Few in numbers, the Palaro warriors compensated for this weakness by bravery and skill. Many of their songs reflect their preoccupation with this problem:

Palaro gin acel, aryo,	*The host of Palaro, only a few, you can count them,*
Otingo polo ki tere;	*Lifted the sky from its base;*
Ee, Lango ringo,	*Ee, the Lango fled;*
Otingo polo ki tere;	*They lifted the sky from its base*
Palaro gin acel, aryo,	*The host of Palaro, only a few, you can count them,*

Payira, the most powerful chiefdom, at least in terms of numbers, advanced against Palaro. In the next poem, the warriors of Palaro taunt the giant, 'Come on, do not fear':

Payira mito lworo,	*Payira seems overwhelmed by fear,*
Abok oywayo mony tero kom Palaro;	*Abok leads his host against Palaro;*
Payira wek lworo;	*Payira, stop your fears;*
Payira, Palaro otoro komgi,	*Payira, Palaro have closed their ranks;*
Payira mito lworo.	*Payira seems overwhelmed by fear.*

The warriors of Puranga had massed at the foot of Omoro hill, in readiness to launch an invasion on a Palaro clan. But the attack never came. The invaders melted away; and a Palaro poet retorted:

Puranga, wek lworo obedi;	*Puranga, leave your cowardliness;*
Lwak pa Lutara-moi peke.	*The army of Lutaramoi has vanished.*
Ee, cunya mito lemma ye,	*Ee, I feel like vomiting, oh,*
O, mony oran te Omoro,	*O, the army has melted away under Omoro hill,*
Puranga mito nywaro jo.	*The warriors of Puranga wish to insult us.*

In the battle of the bamboo forest, the Palaro, led by Agola, dealt a heavy defeat on the Padibe; Piribong, who commanded the Padibe army, was killed, and the remnants of his men fled, leaving his corpse in the dust:

Kakare rac,	*The place was awful,*
Coo lal i koo;	*Men perished in the bamboo forest;*
Padibe, coo lal i koo;	*Men of Padibe perished in the bamboo forest,*
Coo olal i koo do nye,	*Men perished in the bamboo forest, o yes,*
Coo otum bot Piribong,	*Piribong's men were finished,*
Piribong odong i apulu . . .	*And Piribong was left in the dust . . .*

In the next song, the warriors of Palaro chased an unnamed army down the hill. It is clear that the invaders had planned a surprise attack, but the Paipeno clan of Palaro were ready when they came:

Ongai ringo ki bere alunga do;	*Ongai flees, his flag sloping, oh;*
Paipeno oling kim got,	*Paipeno are silent on the hillside;*
Ka ongeyo kome;	*They are aware;*
Jo Paipeno oling kim got	*Paipeno are silent on the hillside,*
Ka ongeyo kome;	*They are aware;*
Obot ka ongeyo kome,	*Obot is aware;*
Obot ka ongeyo kome;	*Obot is aware,*
Ongai ringo ki bere alunga	*Ongai flees, his flag sloping!*

The history of Palaro chiefdom is primarily the story of the various commoner clans, loosely associated with the chief's clan. Most of the battles fought were clan battles, rather than chiefdom ones. It is difficult to arrange the poems in any chronological order.

The history of Paimol chiefdom from Omol, the founder, to 1918, when their chief Lakidi was hanged by the British colonial authorities, was always a turbulent story. Omol, from whom the chiefdom derived its name, jumped the Nile from Bunyoro at Wang wat Pajao, the present Murchison Falls. After a short sojourn among the Payira, he pushed eastwards until he reached Akwang hill, where his people have settled ever since. He found the Acut people on top of the hill; they had climbed there to escape from Jie raids. Omol invited them to come down, and promised them protection; they in turn agreed to be ruled by Omol. Other clan groups, some Luo-speaking, others of Jie and Karamojong, also attached themselves to Omol. The Kudeg became the priestly clan.

The *mwoc* of Paimol reflects this interesting mixture of cultural and linguistic groups, for although the people now all speak a Luo dialect, only one line of the *mwoc* is in Luo; all the rest are not only unintelligible to me, but Paimol elders could not tell me what they meant.

> Kutukutu,
> Morogeno,
> Lalangatobong,
> Moro Laiberu,
> *Aya medo kwon*,
> Moro kangatuk,
> Cumatelo.

The italicised line means: Mother, bring some more millet bread.

Omol fought against his brother Okor, to avenge the death of his son Aluka, who was alleged to have been killed by Okor. Okor rejected the charge, and pleaded that Aluka had been killed by a hyena, and he had nothing to do with his death. Omol was not impressed by this argument, and took up his spear against his brother.

Odyek otingo Aluka woko do,	*Hyena has carried Aluka away oh,*
Latin pa Omera,	*Son of my brother,*
Lapaibwor, Langol,	*Man of Paibwor, Langol,*
Mina tong adyeri;	*Give me a spear now;*
Odyek otingo Aluka woko ye;	*Hyena has taken Aluka away, oh;*
Ee, Langol mina tonga ye.	*Ee, Langol, give me a spear, oh.*

Okor and his group were defeated in the ensuing fight; the reason, according to the following song, was that they were numerically inferior:

Ye, atero oneko wod Omolo;	*Oh, an arrow has killed the son of Omoko;*
Nok ocera lweny ye.	*We are only a few, we cannot fight.*

Okor broke away after the defeat, and settled on Opella hill, where some of his descendants, Pukor, are still found today. The five Paimol historical songs that follow refer to events that happened during the reign of Lakidi, their last chief. The first tells of the wars against the neighbouring chiefdom of Kabala. Arab slavers and ivory dealers had arrived and encamped in Kabala territory. They sent a delegation to Paimol to demand supplies of millet. These were driven away with insults. The Arabs then decided to teach the Paimol a lesson. In a combined operation with the Kabala, they inflicted heavy losses in their attack. Three Paimol generals, including Wangale, were killed.

The Paimol had to wait for a whole year before they could have their revenge. The younger men were impatient, but the elders cautioned patience; they knew that an attack on the Kabala when the Arabs were still around would be foolish, in view of the superiority in weapons and number that the enemy enjoyed. But as soon as the Arabs withdrew Lakidi invited their ally, Omiya Pacua, to join them in an attack on the Kabala, and in a major invasion the Kabala were slaughtered in great numbers.

The Paimol battle formation showed influences of the Nilo-Hamitic age-sets system. In front were the *tiria*, the youthful, battle-eager men, between eighteen and thirty years of age. Then came the seasoned warriors called *jo eleki* aged between thirty and fifty. Behind these were the *jo ete*, old men beyond fifty. They surrounded the chief and carried no shields. The next poem cautions patience to the *tiria* : soon the shield provided by the Arabs will be removed, and the enemy will be exposed. Then, the song says, the *tiria* will have their time; in fact they alone will be allowed to do the fighting;

Okelo kome,	*The enemy has exposed his body,*
Adyeri ye,	*I will leave him for you,*
Ee, lwak pa Wangale;	*Oh host of Wangale ;*
Okelo kome te Akwang do;	*The enemy has exposed his body under Akwang hill oh ;*

Tiria balo ki arima;	*Young warriors, do not spoil things with impatience;*
Ee, lwak pa Wangale,	*Ee, host of Wangale,*
Kitino pa Onyang,	*Children of Onyang,*
Nye, gwok wubal ki arima.	*Do not spoil things by impatience.*

The next poem records the victory of the Paimol over the Kabala; it mentions their allies, the Omiya Pacua, and blames the chief of Kabala for having foolishly assisted the Arabs:

Oneko woda ye,	*The enemy killed my son;*
Jo pa Onyang obutu i tim;	*Now the sons of Onyang are scattered in the wilderness;*
Ee, ngwec oloyo ya Kabala.	*Ee, the people of Kabala could not escape*
Onyang yang ajuki kwe;	*Onyang, I did advise you, but you refused;*
Ngwec oloyo kitino pa Onyang,	*Now the sons of Onyang are scattered in the wilderness;*
Yam ajuku degi	*I advised you and you did not hear;*
Kitino Omiya owinyo Paimol;	*The men of Omiya have agreed to help the Paimol;*
Oneko woda.	*He had killed my son.*

In the battle described above, a man of Patongo, who was on a visit to Kabala, was killed. To avenge his death, warriors from Patongo fell on Paimol women who were working in the fields and killed some. The Paimol answered with two raids, killing some men of Patongo. Two poems tell the story. In the first, the Paimol poet posing as a Patongo warrior, complains that their general called Rungula Nyepur was leading them to a sure death, and asks him not to advance:

Rungula Nyepur tero wa do i to;	*Rungula Nyepur leads us to our death;*
Rungula, woda dong i nguny tugu.	*Rungula, my son will die under the barusus palm;*
Gwok ier ali wa ya.	*Do not start a feud,*
Rungala woda dong i ngony tugu;	*Rungula, my son will die under the barusus palm;*
Ii, Akwang ma lakee.	*The spirit Akwang demands human sacrifice.*

In the second attack the Paimol set the Patongo village on fire and many people were killed, as the next song records:

Lweny ma Lenga-moi ywa ye,	*In the battle commanded by Lenga-moi,*
Opo Awai oyango rwot	*Opo Awai skinned the chief*
Ame lee tim;	*Like a wild animal;*
Oboke olwedo mukonye,	*The leaves of the olwedo tree helped him;*
Tong romo ki wedi ye,	*Spears met spears oh,*
Ilamo lapi kwe;	*In vain you invoked your luck;*
Lweny ma Lenga-moi ywa ye,	*In the battle led by Lenga-moi oh,*
Jo Patongo owang i mac	*The people of Patongo were burnt in the fire*
Ame lee tim.	*Like wild beasts.*

Lakidi was executed in 1918, together with three of his generals. Orom and Jie raiders had carried away a number of women, children and stock from Paimol, and Lakidi immediately set afoot plans for an invasion of Orom and Jie. The District Commissioner in Kitgum intervened; but his efforts to persuade Lakidi to accept a peaceful settlement failed. Interpreting this as open 'rebellion' against the colonial authority, Paimol was attacked. By now the warriors of Paimol had acquired considerable firearms from the Arabs. The battle raged for three days. Then the Paimol fighters ran out of ammunition and surrendered. Lakidi escaped, but was captured and hanged. The following song records the painful story:

Iyee, odonyo i Gala;	*Oh, he has surrendered to the white man;*
Ngedamoi, rwot Akwang ngalo to;	*Ngeda-moi, chief of Akwang chides death;*
Rwot Akwang, Ngedamoi we;	*Chief of Akwang, Ngeda-moi, oh;*
Odongo i Gala ye.	*He has surrendered to the white man, oh.*

Mwoc—the praise-name

Mwoc are short poems that an individual shouts at certain critical moments. During a quarrel, when a person is highly provoked, he shouts his *mwoc* and the fight begins at once, and during the fight he shouts his praise-name on hitting or spearing or throwing down his opponent. In a hunt, the *mwoc* is shouted by the person who spears an animal. When playing the hunting game called *lawala*, *mwoc* is shouted when the moving target has been speared. And at the dance an individual shouts his praise-name when he has reached the peak of his enjoyment and pleasure.

There are two kinds of *mwoc*, one which belongs to a particular individual alone, and the other which belongs to the chiefdom. Every Acoli male has his own *mwoc*, and many but not all women have theirs too. It usually arises from some funny incident. Some years back, when I was a small boy, my mother took me on a visit to Pabo. On arrival, our hostess, a woman called Agik, began to prepare food. After cooking the meat, she began to prepare the millet bread. She put the pot of water in the cooking stove, and the water began to boil. She had no flour, but hoped that her co-wife, who had just returned from visiting her mother, might have some. She went to ask this woman but, alas, there was no flour. Agik burst out crying in great shame. So I got my *mwoc* which goes:

Ogeno moko pa nyeke	*She hoped that her co-wife had some flour;*
Iwaci nyeka oa ki Parabongo,	*She saw her co-wife return from Parabongo,*
Okelo moko ki tobi;	*And thought she had brought some flour and yeast;*
Irii tu jwi;	*You visit your home frequently;*
Ipoto we kituti.	*You fall into the inner room, crying.*

A friend and I went to woo a girl .We met her on the way going to fetch water; she took us into her mother's hut, and asked us to wait for her. There were some beans cooking on the stove, and very bitter smoke from the end of the firewood. So my friend tried to stop the smoke by pushing the piece of firewood into the stove, and in so doing, he knocked the pot over. We were all covered with ash. When the girl

168

returned, we did not stay long, because of the shame. Who ever disturbed a cooking pot in his mother-in-law's house? So my friend's *mwoc* goes:

Atuk, otuk ruk;	*I am the one who knocks down, listen to the sound of the pot as it falls;*
Ituku ten iot pa maro;	*You are the one who knocks down cooking pots in the house of the mother-in-law.*
Wi okwor ki buru,	*Your hair is white with ash,*
Ituku ten.	*You are the disturber of the cooking pot.*

Some *mwoc*, however, are comments about the human situation and are more serious. My father's *mwoc* belong to this category:

Lak tar,	*White teeth,*
Lak tar, miyo kinyero wi lobo.	*It is the whiteness of our teeth that makes us laugh in this world;*
Lakwo kidongo to laling.	*A thief is being beaten, they will kill him, but he does not cry aloud.*

In other words, when we laugh, it is not because we are happy, rather it is because we want to show our teeth; and when a thief is caught, he does not make an alarm, as this would call more people to beat him.

Friends refer to each other by their *mwoc*, usually only a word, or a line. Thus I call my friend *Atuk*, and he calls me *Ogeno moko* And one form of greeting among friends is the exchange of the *mwoc*: one shouting the praise-name of the other. So when I meet my friend Ongiya, this is what happens:

Okot:	Atuk, otuk ruk;
Ongiya:	Ogeno moko pa nyeke;
Okot:	Ituku ten i ot pa maro;
Ongiya:	Iwaci nyeki oa Parabongo;
Okot:	Wi okwor ki buru;
Ongiya:	Okelo moko ki boti;
Okot:	Ituku ten;
Ongiya:	Irii tu jwi;
Okot:	Otuk ruk;
Ongiya:	Ipoto wi kituti.

In one sense these personal *mwoc* are not really praise-names at all. They are personal poems, which identify an individual, and play the same role as the individual tunes that each male plays on his horn or trumpet. But, because they are shouted at moments when the individual has achieved something worth being proud of, we may call them praise-names.

The chiefdom *mwoc* is shared by all members of the chiefdom; and is also shouted by wives of that group, except when the situation is such that her loyalty to her people is at stake. Thus, when her brothers have come to visit her husband, and there is a dance, she shouts her people's *mwoc*.

These poems often embody names of chiefs of old, names of mountains and rivers—sites once occupied by the chiefdom, fierce beasts or harmful plants, etc, which are supposed to exhibit or represent the characteristics or quality of the people of the chiefdom; or thus may contain slogans, telling what the chiefdom has been: its strength and glory, etc. The *mwoc* of Atyak chiefdom goes as follows:

Lwani ye,	*Lwani oh,*
Acut ye,	*Acut oh,*
Manyago ye,	*Manyago oh,*
Nyaka Cedo ye,	*The daughter of Cedo oh,*
Ito nyong, aculu ku.	*Your death will not be avenged,*
	I will not pay any compensation.

The first three lines are names of Atyak ancestors; the last lines imply that any attempt by others to avenge the killings inflicted by the powerful Atyak warriors will be repulsed. A genealogical diagram of the aristocratic lineage show where most of the names are derived.

Atyak, the founder of the chiefly clan, had four sons. Lwani succeeded his father, and later his great-grandson Manyago led the people across the Nile into Acoliland from the West Nile. They crossed on papyrus sudd at a place called Coekitimi. The descendants of Acut were also there, but when Manyago and his group had got across, the sudd began to move and the people of Acut were cut off. They returned to Metu hill in Madi country, and assumed the chiefship of the Madi Mujo through marriage with the chief's daughter.

When the Atyak warriors shout the *mwoc* of their chiefdom they mention the three most important names and landmarks in the history of the chiefdom: Lwani, the first ruler after the founder; Many-

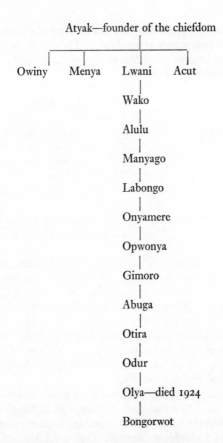

Atyak—founder of the chiefdom

Owiny Menya Lwani Acut

Wako

Alulu

Manyago

Labongo

Onyamere

Opwonya

Gimoro

Abuga

Otira

Odur

Olya—died 1924

Bongorwot

ago who led them across the Nile; the Acut clan, their brothers, who were dramatically cut off for ever by the waters of the Nile. They also boast of the might of the people of Atyak.

For the Payira, the largest chiefdom in terms of territory and population, the source of their glory is the size of the population. They liken their army to the numerous warrior brown ants. During the reign of Onguka, there was minor famine among the Payira. Their neighbours, the Ogom, had grown many pumpkins. Onguka sent for some and he liked them very much; and so he sent for more and more The people of Ogom got fed up with the endless request for pumpkins, and one day they sent the bitter green gourds. Onguka threatened to attack. The Ogom surrendered before a spear was hurled They were 'drunk up' as easily as water, and became a commoner clan of Payira chiefdom. The *mwoc* of Payira records this incident:

Amata ye,	*I drunk you up quickly,*
Olyero ye,	*Clitoris,*
Lyer pa nya Okomo ye,	*Clitoris of the daughter of Okomo;*
Ka lungo mola ye,	*The place where the women adorn themselves with brass ornaments,*
Ka bedo abeda ye,	*The place of leisure;*
Moro ye,	*We are numerous as the warrior brown ants;*
Agwata ma tek mac ma puku	*A hard gourd is softened by fire;*
Amati woko koni.	*I will drink you up now now.*

'Lyer a meni', 'Your mother's clitoris', is the bitterest and most provocative insult. It invariably sparks off an immediate fight. In the *mwoc*, the Payira imply that they can afford to insult anybody's mother; for who dares start a fight against such a mighty army? Moreover, peace being ensured by the large and invincible army, women of Payira spend their time adorning themselves with brass ornaments brought home as part of the loot. And any proud chiefdom who dares to attack the Payira would be humiliated, softened, as a hard gourd is softened by fire, and drunk up easily.

Otole and *bwola* songs and the chiefdom *mwoc* are all mnemonics that the Acoli employ as they dance their history; and although no dates are mentioned, when the songs and the *mwoc* are interpreted, a reasonably full history of a chiefdom emerges. They are a kind of running commentary on the history of a chiefdom; more, they express what the people of a chiefdom think and feel about themselves, their past and future. And, as is to be expected, a people's view about themselves is always biased in their own favour. Their failures are minimised and their victories emphasised and exaggerated. Compare, for example, the boasts of the Payira as contained in the *mwoc* above, with what the Labongo chiefdom think about them, as expressed in the poems such as 'Payira seems overwhelmed by fear' (74), and 'Aliker, return my cattle' (68). Some chiefdom *mwoc* in the discussion on poets as historians; below are a few more personal and chiefdom *mwoc*.

Personal mwoc

Abaa, nen ka lacan cuna!	*Father, look, this poor man is wooing me!*
Ituru yeca,	*You break my feathers;*
Ijwaya kilong,	*You rub me the wrong way,*
Ituru yeca.	*And break my feathers.*
Del wangi pek pi kwon,	*Your eyelids are heavy because of food;*
Amic, dek oo,	*Amic, as soon as the food arrives,*
Wangi li-cuc,	*Your eyes are darkened,*
Wangi col pi dyang oree.	*Your eyes are dark,*
	because of the meat of the cow which died of dysentery.
Dako boli,	*A woman throws you down;*
Dako kali ki nyango;	*A woman jumps over you in the morning;*
Okutu oryang oyeco iti;	*The horns of the oryang tree have torn your ears.*
Apua boyo won ot.	*The husband is covered in dust.*
Wegi mon i obot pul;	*Married men collect and eat the remnants of ground nuts, after the harvest;*
Won laa giliri	*The man wearing the fox-skin*
Ocodo ratili.	*Has broken the weight-measure.*
Kicaa taa pari nono;	*Your tobacco bag is ever empty;*
Iyeng ki olel anyiri;	*Your stomach bulges after eating the soup of the edible rat;*
Aryo-adek kany gang pa maro	*Every now and then you are at your mother-in-law's home.*

Chiefdom mwoc
Patiko

Kweya yee,	*I will cool you down, oh;*
Ager yee,	*I am fierce, oh;*
Ngu yee,	*I am a lion, oh;*
Otigo ma nok tyeko kwon;	*A little dish of lady's finger finishes a whole loaf of millet bread;*
Konni akweyi woko koni.	*In a moment I will cool you down.*

The next form of chiefdom praise is a marching song called *wayu*.

La-lak tongwa do,	*He is for the blades of our spears, oh;*
Wan Patiko wacamo kalara	*We men of Patiko,*
Warubu ki nyige;	*We eat hot pepper together with its seeds;*
Ee, eiya;	*Ee, ee;*
Morongole, eiya,	*Morongole, ee,*
Morongole, ee,	*Morongole, ee,*
La-lak tongwa.	*He is for the blades of our spears.*

Padibe

Ogul mola yee;	*Brass armlets oh;*
Kamlara yee;	*Hot pepper oh;*
Kitetta yee;	*We are like the hottest peppers oh;*
Aceba yee;	*Aceba* oh;*
Pater-lac yee;	*Pater-lac,† oh;*
Puribiribi yee;	*We make the enemy run, oh.*

Labongo

Kilakaci yee;	*Kilakaci‡ oh;*
Mwani yee;	*Mwani§ oh;*
Leng tenge,	*Withdraw and move away,*
Wek ki abaa;	*Leave the fight to my father;*
Gem yee	*We are mean, oh;*
Lamit yee.	*Lamit¶ oh.*

The Acoli also have praise-names for certain items of nature. I give two examples: rain and elephant.

When it is raining hard, and the lightning is flashing and it is thundering threateningly, the old man in the house says the following:

Olim lim,	*Bringer of wealth,*
Opit kic;	*Feeder of orphans,*
Cwee mot;	*Fall gently;*
Bi ipit wa mot;	*Come and feed us peacefully;*
Cwee giri mot.	*Oh fall gently.*

---

* Aceba was the second chief of Padibe, after the founder of the chiefdom called Dibe, who gave the chiefdom its name.
† Pater-lac was the third chief of Padibe.
‡ and § I was not able to discover what these terms meant.
¶ Lamit is the palace of Labongo chiefs.

When an elephant trumpets in the distance, or is spotted a long way away, the hunter says the following:

Luwau,	*The tall one,*
Lucoro oboke,	*The shaker of leaves,*
Lunima-nima,	*The one that walks heavily,*
Lim dog	*Having a good appetite,*
Oweko adongo ma dit.	*That is why I have grown big.*

Warrior's Titles

I who overthrew the foe
returned to the fight
as they attacked us

I who surprised the foe
went ahead of those not yet in the fight

Bahima: Ebyevugo

Bwanga-moi	*One who throws only one spear and puts the enemy to flight.*
Muku-moi	*One who kills a man and a boy.*
Ladwe-moi	*One who kills by moonlight.*
Mulu-moi	*One who kills a cripple; One who kills an enemy who is crawling away.*
Atula-moi	*One who kills by night when the owls cry.*
Munga-moi	*One who kills secretly; whose deed is not celebrated.*
Lumany-moi	*One who kills secretly and destroys the evidence of the deed.*
Anyanga-moi	*One who kills with a newly forged spear, the shaft of which is still light-coloured.*
Aliro-moi	*One who spears an enemy who is prevented from falling by the spear which props the body.*
Adar-moi	*The ambusher, one who lies in wait.*
Abel-moi	*One who puts the enemy to flight.*
Agel-moi	*One who kills the enemy's flank man.*
Acura-moi	*One who kills by throwing the spear towards the enemy, but without aiming at a particular body.*

Angolo-moi	*One who cuts off and kills the leading man of an invading party*
Aleko-moi	*One who captures an enemy by warding him off with his spearshaft from the men on his side, saying, 'This is my war captive.'*
Ayuto-moi	*One who takes a prisoner and runs off with him, leaving the battle.*
Abal-moi	*One who kills a woman.*
Angiya-moi	*One who expressly chooses out a particular enemy in battle, but while he is spying him out someone else slays that enemy.*
Arima otum	*One who throws a spear and then runs somewhere else to throw another from a safe distance, for fear of reprisals.*
Adila-moi	*One who kills early in the morning.*
Anyeko	*One who captures a woman.*
Alal-moi	*One who kills during the pursuit of a routed enemy.*
Akul-oling	*One who kills the owner of a kraal.*
Apenyo-moi	*One who kills an enemy after teasing him, saying, 'Today, you will not escape.'*
Akumatum	*One who kills an old man.*
Arengo-moi	*One who kills an enemy after hunting him out of the main body.*
Adiyo-moi	*One whose captive is killed by someone else, while the captive is asking for mercy, and is considering the matter with his spear-point pressed against the captive's chest.*
Alira-moi	*One who runs an enemy to a standstill and then makes him a prisoner.*
Aluko-moi	*One who kills on the way home from a raid.*

Alengo-moi	One who kills a man on the road and then hides the body in the grass alongside.
Atyera-moi	One whose spearshaft breaks on piercing the enemy's body.
Awira-moi	One who escorts a visitor and then kills him.
Apelo-moi	One who spears an enemy who runs away, wounded.
Anyap-moi	One who kills with a spear whose shaft is clumsy and heavy.
Atyam-moi	One who kills a blind man.
Abalo-moi	One whose spearshaft breaks during its flight.
Apena-moi	One who selects a particular enemy, identifying him by some ornament, and saying, 'I claim that man with the brass wire.'
Akakocal	One who participates in a drawn battle.
Akor-moi	One who keeps stabbing a dead man.
Adya-moi	The lucky man who is constantly missed by the enemy.
Abura-moi	One who kills without delay.
Ayok	A coward who keeps pretending to throw his spear, but does not.
Awany-moi	One who, being a guest in a village, joins a raid, and kills a man.
Ayo-ngwe-moi	A man who kills a man on the road and leaves him there.
Akango-moi	One who kills a starving enemy.
Ariyu-moi	One who kills an enemy and stretches him along the path.
Adwe-moi	One who boasts that he kills every full moon.

Index of titles in Acoli

Index of titles in English